Robert Cremins

Robert Cremins was born in 1968 in Dublin. He was educated at Trinity College and the University of East Anglia. He lives in Texas with his wife and their two sons. His first novel *A Sort of Homecoming*, is also available as a Sceptre Lir paperback.

PRAISE FOR *A Sort of Homecoming*

'The funniest novel I have read all year' *Observer*

'Nobody sees his land as mercilessly objectively, and sentimentally subjectively, as a self-exiled young native son on his return. He writes very well' *Irish Times*

ROBERT CREMINS

To Glenda and Terry —

Send in the Devils

Welcome to my Texas.

Robert Cremins

S

SCEPTRE
LIR

Copyright © 2001 by Robert Cremins

First published in Great Britain in 2001 by Hodder and Stoughton
A division of Hodder Headline

The right of Robert Cremins to be identified as the Author
of the Work has been asserted by him in accordance with the
Copyright, Designs and Patents Act 1988.

A Sceptre Lir paperback

1 3 5 7 9 10 8 6 4 2

A CIP catalogue record for this title
is available from the British Library

ISBN 0 340 71726 2

Printed and bound in Great Britain by
Mackays of Chatham plc, Chatham, Kent

Hodder and Stoughton
A division of Hodder Headline
338 Euston Road
London NW1 3BH

To Melanie

devil: [n]

1. A malignant or wicked person.

2. One who does work for which another receives the credit.

3. A wretch.

It is a spot on God's Earth that, once seen, is not easily relinquished.

– from the original prospectus for the City of Maverick, 1841

Part One

DUBLIN

What is John Paul Mountain, of all people, doing in Maverick, Texas?

That was the question I had heard constantly around Dublin for two years, accompanied by no end of answers. Nobody was happy with the official story, the authorised version brought back from his wedding: John Paul selling *cars*?

The son of pundits, scion of Ireland's first media family, he had been raised to sell nothing but himself. Within a few years of spinning out of Trinity, John Paul had failed to make it as a frontman, film-maker, and poet-provocateur. He was famous for not being famous.

So America we could understand – America was always the end-logic of those fizzled vocations – but Maverick wasn't that kind of America, was it? Nobody from Dublin had ever been there before the wedding.

Marrying into money also made sense. He had come from money and now returned to it, like a homecoming. And everyone, even his many enemies, expected that he would take some time out from Dublin after his *annus horribilis* – death of mother, disgrace of father, rift with sister, embarrassment of self. Week after week he was caught in the triangulations of gossip created by the *Sunday Sybarite*'s star hacks. A year in the East Village or Barcelona or even Borneo was clearly on the cards. But Texas . . . Texas was taking it too far.

And so the rumours sprouted like fungi:

John Paul was writing a memoir about the tasty chaos of his

family life; John Paul was dead, having crashed his Lamborghini on an LA freeway; John Paul was alive and well and living in Dublin under an assumed name – Tom Iremonger swore he'd had a drink with him at four o'clock in the morning in a basement club on Leeson Street.

These reports were all plausible (this was John Paul Mountain we were talking about), and I believed none of them. Instead I had this tenacious inkling that the truth was messier, muddier than anyone suggested. If I knew the Mountains at all, it was.

And who am I, you might ask, to be speaking with such authority about a family not my own? Peter Dagg – a pleasure. I had been to school with John Paul (Berchmans, Jesuits), then college (Trinners, atheists), and now I was marrying his sister. Yes, I was engaged to Suzette Mountain. Forget my precocious legal achievements; this was the coup of my life.

More than anyone else, Suzette was determined to bring John Paul back to Dublin, to bring him back to his senses. But she couldn't possibly go to Maverick; her brother would barely speak to Suzette on the phone. And her father couldn't conceivably go. For Jerry Mountain, Ireland's erstwhile swinging politician, was afraid to fly.

We were finishing lunch in Collegium (Daire ffrench-Brady's third new restaurant of the year), on the eastern fringe of Temple Bar.

'Why me?' I asked.

'Because he respects you,' Suzette replied.

'John Paul respects *me*?'

'Of course. Deep down he'd like to be doing what you're doing, instead of being stuck' – she waved vaguely westward – 'out there. He wants a normal life, our kind of normal. It's his pride that's getting in the way, Peter. He's made a terrible choice and he'd rather wallow in it than admit he's made a mistake and come back to Dublin like any reasonable person.'

I twiddled my empty wine glass.

4

'You haven't by any chance considered the possibility, Suzette dearest, that he might actually be . . . happy in Maverick?'

She was not amused. Leaning over the remnants of her crab and tomato risotto, she told me, 'I know my brother, Peter. He's a Mountain. He has to be saved from himself now and then.' That observation did make her smile.

'So this isn't just about the wedding.'

She shook her head. 'Sweetie, this wedding isn't just about you and me.'

'Of course not, of course not,' I nodded sadly, prodding my rocket salad.

Our table was beside the snaking black railings of the mezzanine. On the museum-white walls (and to think only the year before the place had been a clerical outfitters) were a quartet of vampire portraits by Sam Hardiman, the kind that rival restaurants had been found guilty of faking.

Nothing untoward was happening in the canvases – the subjects were between meals – but still they had me feeling a little queasy about Daire's food. Not that I mentioned that to my fiancée. She was his publicist, and he was one of the few clients she'd managed to keep for more than a few months. Suzette, though she didn't quite know it herself, had a natural talent for rubbing people the wrong way, but her quixotic career choice made me think of her all the more tenderly.

There was now a classic Dublin quid pro quo going on: Daire was catering our big day – a coup in itself – for a not too obscene sum of money; in return Suzette was giving him a year's worth of free public relations, a currency whose value I still had my (unprofessed) doubts about. A bargain, by any standards.

'Well?' Suzette prompted me; I was merely toying with my food now; she was finished with hers. I responded with a deliberate sigh:

'Suzette, love, with all due respect, it's a crazy idea. Utter folly.

For a start, I'm swamped with work. I was up at five this morning working on that leave for judicial review.'

This was no exaggeration. The new money had made Dubliners wonderfully litigious. When divorce really got going I would have to invent another Peter Dagg, Junior Counsel, to handle all the work.

'But Peter, sweetie, I wouldn't dream of asking you now. I meant the summer.'

The summer. She had me there, and we both knew it. In the summer, we barristers become artificially unemployed: the Law Library closes for two months, August and September. Normally I don't mind, I don't mind at all. It's like being in school still and getting your summer hols. In fact, that's one of the things that attracted me to the legal profession. But now my free summer, the last one before marriage and mortgage, was under assault. I got just the tiniest bit stroppy:

'Why can't we just leave him be? Mmn? I'm sure John Paul will come round in his own time. In his own time, Suzette.'

She matched my mood. 'And will my father still be alive when he does? Peter, I think he's being about as honest with me about his health as he was at the tribunal about his Bermuda bank accounts.'

This is what she was talking about:

At the MacVerry Tribunal, Jerry had almost got away with his denials that he'd ever trafficked in influence, until copious evidence of his off-shore wealth was mysteriously deposited in a bin on Liffey Street. Twice the Director of Public Prosecutions brought a case against him, and twice the former minister was found not guilty. The sickly witness he made for on the stand had something to do with that, but his ill-health was not an act. Now his colon cancer was, allegedly, in remission. And because Suzette had brought that subject up, I just couldn't act the lawyer. So, going – reluctantly – against my training, I asked a question I knew she would have a compelling answer to:

6

'Why not send one of JP's real friends?'

'But that's exactly the point,' she replied, leaning so earnestly towards me she got some basil mousse on her blouse. 'Don't you see? I wouldn't dream in a million years of asking one of his old crowd to take this on. They did absolutely nothing to convince him to mend fences when he met them in Paris last summer, so I don't see any of them doing much better over there. It would be like his wedding all over again. Apparently they did nothing but guzzle margaritas and tell him that he's on the pig's back in Texas. What am I going to do, give Tom *Iremonger* the job? Peter, this has to be done, and somebody responsible has to do it.'

I pinned a half-smile on my face. 'And responsibility means me.'

Suzette smiled fully. 'I take that to be a yes.'

I took off my compact horn-rimmed glasses and cleaned them with my handkerchief. (I think I am the only man of my generation to carry one.) 'You can take that as a we'll see,' I muttered.

Suzette glowed. 'Do you have time to share a slice of that amaretto chocolate torte? Daire makes it himself.'

I glanced at my watch, brushed my mouth with the purple serviette, and shook my head apologetically.

'Sorry, sweetie, but I really should be somewhere else.'

There was a time when I was not in such demand.

A September evening, the early weeks of my final year in Berchmans. Myself and two classmates, with whom I regularly walked down to the bus, were leaving the changing rooms after rugby practice. The tarmac around us was strewn with the Swiss-cheese slices of dried mud from a hundred boots. Colley and Butler were on the Firsts and I was on the Thirds, but the mere fact that I played, that I went out to practise, made me tolerable.

John Paul Mountain, a fifth year, came out of the sixth-year cottage. John Paul didn't play; he was beyond rugby. Every item of his Berchmans uniform was stylised, not quite regulation – the trousers cuffed, the jumper a darker shade of blue. He'd lost the tie; I'd put mine back on. John Paul's urbanity was compromised by long, thin arms he hadn't yet grown into. But the glassy, disturbing eyes – his mother's eyes – were already working their mature effect.

'How come you're here so late, John Paul?' Butler asked politely.

'Detention,' John Paul said, as if stating the obvious. Detention was his nurturing mother. 'You fellows mind if I walk down with you?'

Did we mind? Not at all.

'Where's your bike, John Paul?' asked Colley.

All of Berchmans knew about his bike – a limited edition Peugeot twenty-speed, reputedly the only one of its kind in the country.

John Paul Mountain shrugged. 'A little mishap on the dual carriageway.'

I was neither in nor out of the freewheeling, profane conversation that developed as we walked down the avenue. When the others stopped to buy cigarettes at the garage on the main road I bought strong mints, though I really wanted something sweeter. We turned onto Fitzwilton Road, John Paul's road. Looking at the tall red-brick façades I saw lords and ladies turning up their noses. Colley and Butler were smoking John Paul's Marlboros.

We reached St Cloud or, as Berchmans boys called it, the Cloud House. John Paul stopped by the smaller gate; we stopped.

'An espresso would go well with this,' he sighed at his cigarette.

I wasn't quite sure what an espresso was. It sounded as exotic as hash.

'Why don't you fellows come in?' He was looking at his fellow smokers only. Despite their attempt at nonchalance, I could tell that they thought admittance into the Cloud House a treat.

But what was I, the uninvited, to do? The few times John Paul had acknowledged my existence at school he had not acted with direct disdain, as I had seen him do with other boys, but that was no guarantee he would not cold-shoulder me once we reached the front door. Perhaps it would be better to cut my social losses, to make some excuse, and continue on my own down the long road to the bus stop outside St Attracta's Church. I couldn't risk humiliation.

The lads were now looking at me with low-key scornful amusement. Don't take this personally, they were saying, but it is a delicious situation. I turned to John Paul to mutter my excuse.

'And would you like to come in, too, Peter?' he said, smiling reasonably, before I had a chance. His timing was suspiciously good.

So all four of us went up the gravel path to the steep steps of the Cloud House. It was semi-detached like my house, but also one half of a three-storey Victorian mansion. The front garden was a miniature Versailles.

Taking their cue from John Paul, the lads kept their cigarettes lit. On the porch he turned to us.

'Use the boot scraper, boys. It's not just an antique.' And he was, in his own light way, dead serious.

As he unlocked the thick green front door, I looked at the intricate, vegetative stained-glass panels on either side. My father referred to Jerry and Nessa Mountain as 'those awful people', but he would have had to admit that they were awful people living in a splendid house.

Carvings and stucco sprouted out of the gloom of the hallway. John Paul led us past high-ceilinged rooms moored by solid, exquisite furniture. You couldn't put your hand on anything that was not of value. And that, I knew, was the famous Nessa Mountain touch. The artwork was abstract and aggressive. I didn't know what it was trying to say, but it did say a lot about the confidence of the people who had put it on their walls.

We followed John Paul down a sharp staircase to the right, into the kitchen. Two girls in the turquoise uniform of the Siena Academy were sitting across from each other at the grand slab of a wooden table, their heads tilted over earthy mugs of coffee, between them a plate of nut-topped brownies.

One, blonde with a wide, rubbery face, looked up; the other, dark as John Paul, looked over a petite shoulder. Her large, dark eyes fixed on me momentarily, then, turning in her chair a little and revealing small, insistent breasts, took in the lads. At last, Suzette.

When the Mountains were featured in the *Sunday Sybarite*'s 'Family Ties' series, I had carefully torn out the article, mostly for the moody black-and-white group portrait featuring slim Suzette in her Gothic finery. Now here she was in the flesh. I felt compelled to do something, anything, that would make me look equal to the other Berchmans boys John Paul had brought home, the Firsts.

Even as I did it, I knew that it was a stupid move, an idiotic gesture, but still I did it, I couldn't help myself: I loosened my Berchmans tie – not much, just a jab to the right, but enough to send the girls caving into each other in fits of giggles.

John Paul and the lads traded slow smirks. I could feel my cheeks flame. It would have been better after all to have headed for the bus stop.

As she would again years later and thousands of miles away, Nessa Mountain saved me.

She appeared midway on the kitchen stairs, a pair of chic reading glasses propped up on her tied-back hair, her face a well-made mask of surprise. 'Well, well, what a party we have going on here,' she said, with a little too much ironic gusto. I wondered if she had been drinking. I'd heard things at Berchmans, even the word *alco*.

She tottered down the final few steps. The lads were looking around meekly for ashtrays, not quite believing that it was OK to smoke in front of a parent, even this peculiar parent.

But John Paul continued to draw leisurely on his Marlboro, smiling flirtatiously at his mother. I couldn't believe that the most fantastical whisperings I had ever heard at Berchmans – to the effect

10

that John Paul Mountain was a little too fond of his mother – were being given some substance here in the Cloud House.

Nessa paid none of the smokers any attention. She walked over to Suzette and her friend. 'Now, girls, are you ready?' She sounded more English than Irish.

Her daughter didn't. 'Yeah,' she replied, glancing over at me, at me specifically, with a smile. She was still savouring the tie incident. But was there more to it than that? Had she truly noticed me?

Her friend had turned more serious. Nessa had taken out a large bunch of keys from the slim handbag she carried on her shoulder. Perhaps the other girl was concerned about being driven by someone under the influence.

Suzette grabbed a tote bag from one of the rustic chairs, and her turquoise friend retrieved her canvas school bag, its neat graffiti featuring the names of safe alternative bands. Nessa turned as she walked towards the glazed side door and said, 'John Paul, sweetheart, I hope you're using the Venezuelan beans for that coffee.'

'Of course, Nessa,' he replied.

Calling your mother by her first name . . . it was unnatural.

So the women left – we heard Nessa's car back out busily down the gravel drive. We sat at the table the girls had abandoned, digging into the brownies they hadn't touched, drinking the Venezuelan coffee. It was far too rich for my taste; then again, I had never been offered anything but instant in a friend's house; then again, this was no regular friend.

Mostly we talked about – or the others talked about – Suzette's friend, Blanaid, the blonde, but I knew Suzette was on the lads' minds too. They were just wary of expressing those desires in front of John Paul. And that made me want her even more.

The conversation turned safe, turned to music, and Butler was astonished when John Paul casually mentioned that he possessed an original copy of the first Velvet Underground album, and that the

Warhol banana on the gatefold cover was unpeeled. 'It's Jerry's, in fact,' he added modestly. 'C'mon on, I'll show you.'

We followed him through the house to a long room next to the conservatory. Here Nessa's touch could not be felt. It was a teenaged space, full of gadgetry and floppy furniture, some of which looked like cast-offs from other rooms, other decorating phases. The blobs inside a glowing purple lava lamp collapsed and refashioned themselves. John Paul sat down and swivelled languorously in a white ball-chair.

In that room I saw my first CD player and first heard the new infallible sound. The lads and I also examined the vintage vinyl collection. At my house you would never have confused one of my records with my father's, but here some of the coolest albums bore the faint signature of Jerry Mountain.

Suddenly in walked the Procul Harem fan. The minister was wearing one of his trademark Kildare Bros. suits, its dark glinting fabric tailored to sharp perfection. In his right hand was a dark green leather briefcase with a gold harp. He held it in the same way I'd seen him carry a cardboard portfolio of smoked salmon down Grafton Street last Christmas Eve: two insouciant fingers hooked around the handle.

I was the first to stand up; Colley and Butler then got to their gawky feet. I assumed John Paul would get up and turn down the Jesus and Mary Chain CD – that crystal-clear cacophony – but he didn't; he just sank back further into the ball-chair. I was tempted to turn down the volume myself. The minister turned it off.

I had seen Jerry Mountain many times before – especially on television, of course – but he had never seen me. He made up for it now, extending a long Mountain arm, focusing on me with a stare and a smile that transformed me, for an instant that begged repeating, into an interesting, significant person, worthy of knowing.

'Jerry Mountain – and you are?'

'Oh, I'm Peter Dagg.'

I shook his hand as confidently as I could. His presence was forceful, honed, American. Television didn't do him justice. Something had arrived in Ireland with Jerry Mountain, something that we – my generation – needed to flaunt, emulate. This man needed to be taoiseach, president. The office that this man needed didn't even exist under our iron-grey constitution. Why had they made him only Minister for Science, Innovation, and Fisheries?

Well, for a start, his party, the Serious Radicals, were the most junior of junior partners in that year's coalition.

'And where do you live, Peter?'

'Owenstown Hill – we all do.'

It was two miles away, it was a hundred miles away.

The minister turned his special attention to my neighbours.

Only when we were on the bus home did I remember that the three of us were his future constituents, the virgin voters of the next general election. Owenstown Hill was a dull gem for the Dinner Party (as the Rads had been irresistibly dubbed). But that was perfect. Not only would I vote for Jerry Mountain, I would campaign for him too. Perhaps that way I would get to see more of his daughter. And less of my family.

My father's chief passions in life were brass rubbings and farmhouse cheeses. The most outrageous thing I had ever known him to do was walk backwards down a stretch of Dun Laoghaire pier to embarrass me. Like Jerry Mountain he was a solicitor; they had been rough contemporaries at Blackhall Place, where my father had known the younger man enough to dislike him. But while Jerry had gone on to bigger and, to my mind, better things, my father had slogged away as a solicitor, building a decent practice, even serving an uneventful term as the President of the Law Society. My mother was tentatively artistic, exhibiting her West of Ireland watercolours once or twice a decade. I had a flotilla of older sisters, two of whom were already married to solicitors.

Sitting upstairs at the very back of that foggy-windowed Bom-bardier bus, heady with second-hand smoke and fresh memories of the Cloud House, I did not feel as if I was going home again.

It would be several years before I learned that Nessa Mountain too had grown up in Owenstown Hill. Her father was a senior civil servant – Permanent Under-Secretary of some department or other – one of the men who had soberly built the Irish Free State. In his spare time, however, Dennis Kelly indulged a bohemian bent (jazz clarinet, apparently, was his release), a tendency he further encouraged in his daughter and only child. Quietly, he made sure that the parish priest gave his blessing to Nessa's desire to study at Trinity, at the dawn of the Sixties still a stronghold of West Britishness, or still perceived to be so.

The parish priest's preferred university, UCD, had not yet moved to the cold comfort of its suburban campus, so Nessa's future husband was studying at the other end of Grafton Street. The mythic meeting – well, mythic in Mountain circles – soon took place in Bewley's Oriental Café.

Jerry was also the son of a civil servant, but nothing so mandarin as a Departmental Permanent Under-Secretary. Jeremiah Mountain, Jr, grew up on the South Circular Road and was educated by the Christian Brothers. A very bright boy – nobody ever doubted Jerry's native intelligence – he won a scholarship to UCD, becoming the first person in his family to attend college.

He soon made a name for himself, and not just because of his gorgeous West Brit of a girlfriend. As a dance promoter, show-band crooner, and soap-box opportunist Jerry made his mark, even if that mark was a stain in some people's eyes. In his final year he was narrowly beaten in the election for auditor of the L and H Debating Society. This did not discourage him. Sure, hadn't the exact same thing happened to James Joyce?

Meanwhile, Nessa's own career was taking off. She immersed

herself in French, spending as much time as possible in Paris, staying with old friends of her parents, the Chenetiers, in their apartment off Avenue Foch.

Under the tutelage of Mme Chenetier, cuisine went from a hobby to a passion, a passion she brought back to Ireland. This was a time when the culinary scene in Dublin did not extend far beyond Jammet's old-school restaurant on Suffolk Street. It was 1962, and Nessa set out to change all that.

Her column in *Trinity News*, 'Nessa's Notes', became popular outside the walls of the college. When she graduated, it graduated with her to the pages of *The Irish Independent*. In turn, that gig landed her a sponsored programme on Radio Eireann, *Cooking with Nessa*. The lack of pictures did not interfere with the show's success. The sound of ingredients being so assertively mixed, together with Nessa's young, clear voice was enough to get the mouth watering. In any case, the pictures soon followed. In 1964 the programme transferred to RTE, the fledging television station, and Nessa became the nation's sweetheart. I've seen some grainy black-and-white footage of the show. Nessa is Jackie Kennedy with an apron, introducing Ireland to some new exotic herb, like basil.

Her marriage to Jerry the following year was the most glamorous event the country had seen since the state visit of Princess Grace. While Jerry was not exactly Prince Ranier, he was a suitable groom. The gossip columnist of one of the evening newspapers had dubbed him 'the solicitor to the stars'. What this meant in reality was that Jerry had recently set up a practice of his own to deal with the modest legal needs of those people who passed for stars in Ireland back then – his bride's Donnybrook colleagues, those pioneering RTE personalities; the odd internationally recognised character actor; a few rugby players.

The ceremony took place in trendy University Chapel, with both private and public photo-calls afterwards across the street in

Stephen's Green. The newly-weds then led the way to the reception at the Shelbourne.

In this fashion Nessa Kelly became Nessa Mountain.

'He blames Jerry for his troubles, he blames me, he blames everybody except the clowns he invited to his wedding,' my fiancée told me as we walked through narrow Merchant's Arch after leaving Collegium, 'but secretly I think he blames himself.'

'Come on,' I snorted.

She stopped at the top of the steps that led down to the quays. We were in people's way, but Suzette didn't seem to notice.

'No, listen, Peter,' she said. 'Some people, when they get in that state, lock themselves away in their room. He's locked himself away in another life.'

'That's a nice theory, my dear.'

'I believe it.' She took a taut breath. 'I also believe we need to do something about it. Before it's too late.'

'And that's why you want me to interfere.'

'That's why I want you to inter*vene*.' She looked away, back into the heart of Temple Bar. 'I don't think I could take another death.'

I looked down at my resoled leather brogues and at Suzette's slim black pumps. My fiancée spent more on shoes than food.

Looking up again I said, 'You'd have to let me do it in my own way. None of this American intervention nonsense. A softly, softly approach is the one that would work with John Paul.'

Her crispest smile. 'I'd have it no other way.'

I kissed her abruptly. 'I'd better get back to work, Suz. I'll phone you tonight.'

'Grand. Peter?' I had already walked down the steps. 'You don't want me to walk down as far as the Courts with you?'

'Don't you have that meeting with the comedians?'

'Yes, I do. At three.'

'I want to hear all about it this evening.'

The little green man was with me and I crossed in a crowd to the Ha'penny Bridge side. Feeling a little guilty – I tended to compartmentalise Suzette, now that I'd won her – I turned around, intending to wave, but she was gone. So I crossed the river, which looked almost blue in the spring sunshine, content to be making my way back to the world of evidence and criminals.

My ambition to become a barrister had come as a surprise to many people, not least John Paul.

I remember meeting him on Grafton Street the day the first round of college place offers was published in *The Irish Times*. By then he had been asked to leave Berchmans after he and three other fifth years had been caught at Heathrow with replica weapons they'd bought on a school trip to Marseilles. (That scandal never made it into the papers; Jerry Mountain was still strong.) He would finish up his education at the Agapé Academy, an experimental school on Morehampton Road run by an ex-Jesuit, who had also been kicked out of Berchmans.

But I was done with school.

'So, Peter, did you get what you wanted?'

'Actually yes I did.'

'UCD?'

'No, Trinity.'

'You Trinity?'

Shy nod from me. He went on. 'Let me take a wild guess – Law.'

Modest nod. A sneer from him. 'Yes, indeed. Peter Dagg, scrum-half and solicitor.'

'Actually John Paul I plan to go onto King's Inns.'

He looked genuinely astonished. 'You, a barrister? Imagine that – the Caution Horse a barrister!' I was flattered that he cared enough about my career choice to be astonished. I was less flattered when he added, 'The Caution Horse thinking on his feet!'

Since we'd got to know each other better – you could almost have called us friends – John Paul had given me that nickname, one that would follow me to college, and take me years to shake off. I didn't know where he got it from, and I didn't know what it literally meant, but I had to admit (to myself) that it was not altogether inappropriate for who I was, at that time. And besides, I do see, when I look unflinchingly in the mirror, that I have a very slightly equine face.

The Law schooled me in confidence, and the first time I had to stand up in court and advocate, something clicked. I think the wig was the catalyst. I love the wig. It will be a sad day when it disappears from the courtroom, as I fear it will. I must have been the only lawyer in my King's Inns class who actually looked forward to ordering his wig from Bertram's of London, and forking over four hundred quid. Wearing my canopy of horsehair, arguing my first motion, my cup overfloweth with confidence. I put the excess into other areas of my life.

That evening, after another day of fussy advocacy in the Four Courts and shrewd research in the Law Library, I joined my old master Maurice Swarbrigg and two solicitors, O'Neill and Mahaffy, for a well-deserved pint in the Mallet. I had done very well at Trinity and King's Inns, but once I'd been called to the Bar it had taken the quietly heroic efforts of my father, and an uncle who was a circuit court judge, to secure my apprenticeship to Maurice Swarbrigg. The Law Library considered devilling for him an honour. He was the ultimate master. For almost two years now I'd been out on my own.

A thin creamy moustache formed itself on Maurice's broad upper lip. He probably knew it was there, but made no effort to wipe it away. Maurice in profile made Rumpole of the Bailey look svelte. He turned his warm, leery face to me.

'Plans for the summer hols, Dagg?'

'Nothing definite, Maurice.'

He raised his fat, sparse eyebrows.

'Anything *in*definite?'

Chortles from O'Neill and Mahaffy.

I smiled. 'Might be going over to the States for a while, actually.'

'Summer job?' he jabbed.

'Now that wouldn't be legal, Maurice.'

'Why would that stop you?' He was serious this time.

I sighed. 'Actually, I think I've done enough grunt work this year to keep the wolf from the door till the new session.'

'The divorce is marvellous,' said O'Neill.

'Marvellous altogether,' agreed Mahaffy.

Swarbrigg's eyes locked on mine.

'So why are you going to the States, Peter, if we're allowed to know?'

'Oh, you're allowed to know. I need a little New York in my system, that's all.'

'Any plans to travel on from there?'

I nodded. 'California.'

'And nowhere in between?'

Here I could have lied. But lying – simple honest lying – was not part of the game.

'No solid plans. Why do you ask?'

Maurice replied, 'Well, if my American geography serves me right, equidistant from New York and California would be . . . Maverick, Texas.'

He pronounced the name of the place in such a way as to make it clear that he would never consider going there himself.

I replied, 'Your geography is better than mine.'

He was not distracted. 'No plans to visit the future brother-in-law?'

19

I checked on O'Neill and Mahaffy. They were loving this, soaking it up. This was as good as catching Maurice torturing some poor punter in the Four Courts. But if this was torture, it was torture of the most constructive kind. Every minute spent with Maurice Swarbrigg, SC, was an education. In a way, I was still his devil.

I answered the question with a question:

'Have you been talking to his sister, or his father?'

Maurice's eyebrows rippled.

'My dear Peter, I've been talking to *you*. And look what you have told me.'

I pursed my lips, reckoning. At this stage it would be more interesting to confess.

'Well, it's true Suzette does want me to go out and see him.'

'To what end, might I ask?'

I savoured a sigh.

'To convince him to come home, at least for the wedding.'

O'Neill and Mahaffy exchanged sceptical looks and gurglings. They knew the funeral story. I didn't know anybody in Dublin who didn't know the funeral story. Even the most conservative version of it had Suzette smothering her brother's fist as it flew towards their father, as they stood outside the columbarium where their mother's ashes had just been inserted.

The goal that I'd described – of bringing that violent exile home – must have seemed to those seasoned solicitors as achievable as leading Maurice Swarbrigg through the eye of a needle.

But Maurice himself was thinking.

'Just for the wedding?'

I shrugged briskly. 'As far as I know, just for the wedding. Just for a start.'

'Ah, the *reconciliation*.' He took slow delight in the absurdity of the word.

I snorted as I drank some more of my overpriced German lager.

'That may be too grand a word for it, Maurice. I think Suzette would be happy for John Paul just to be in the same room as them without shouting and the other usual Mountain theatrics.'

Maurice grimaced. 'The columbarium incident,' he said regretfully.

'The columbarium indeed,' I said.

O'Neill and Mahaffy nodded. The Mountains had managed to make columbarium a household word, in roomy Dublin households.

Maurice sat back in his chair, almost capsizing it. He had got it out of me. But Maurice always got it out of you, in the end. The only thing to do was to be a sporting kind of mouse while he pawed you.

'So Suzette thinks you're the right man for the job.'

'Apparently.'

'And do you think you're the right man for the job?'

I took my time answering.

'You know . . . I think I am, Maurice.'

Smacking his lips after a long sip of Guinness – thickening that snowy moustache – and nodding at his drink, not me, he replied:

'Well, you certainly have done your homework on that family. Young Suzette especially.'

O'Neill and Mahaffy cackled, thinking Maurice was making some kind of sexual pun. (If they only knew the truth about Suzette and me and what we hadn't been up to.) Perhaps Maurice was. In any case, I couldn't have cared less about what they thought now. In his rummy way, Maurice Swarbrigg, SC, had issued a professional challenge. The John Paul Mountain case he found intriguing, and since he couldn't take the brief himself, he wanted to see what his pale protégé could do with it, how I would handle it, if I could handle it.

As soon as I got home, I would phone Suzette and give her the definite answer she hadn't got out of me by the Ha'penny Bridge.

I finished up my pint quickly. The conversation meandered into other gossip, other reports. I stood up. Maurice looked up.

'Throwing in the towel so soon, young Dagg?'

'Work to do, Maurice. Work to do.'

Yes, we were not having sex. What was worse, I knew our friends and family suspected. There had been comments, looks. Jerry, I'm sure, was horrified by his daughter's behaviour, but he would have been the last person to bring up the subject of abstinence. And it was at her insistence that we were waiting until we got married, and got married in the church. You see, this was Suzette's rebellion. In reaction to his upbringing, her brother had fled to Maverick. She had stayed put, and retreated from her parents' values (if that's the right word to use for those fashionable shenanigans). It was safe to say that Suzette was the only Dubliner involved in public relations who attended the Tridentine Mass.

And sex? Well, like many a saint, Suzette had been a very active player in that field – and had now renounced all her libertine ways. Which was all very well for her, but think of me, only two girlfriends away from virginity, finally having captured the prize of my sexual dreams or, more to the point, not having captured it. In this matter, I was not the cautious one, but Suzette had insisted on maintaining her virtual virginity. What else could I do but propose marriage? But if people only knew why I had done so. Suzette Mountain, child of Irish modernity, had given me a secret bond with my chaste forefathers. It was a scandal.

When we got engaged, Suzette wrote to John Paul at his parents-in-law's address, the only one in Maverick she had for him. His response was an e-mail, to me:

To: P_Dagg@hibernia.ie
From: JP@Wingatechevy.com

Subject: Betrothal

Dear Peter,
Congratulations. I wish you every happiness. Unfortunately, I won't be there on the day.

Best,
JP

He must have got my address from a mutual acquaintance. I suspected it was Luke Fortune, the proprietor of Bunny Farrell's, a New-Irish bar in the East Village. Luke retained Suzette as his Dublin PR person, insisting that the odd bold-faced mention she got for him in the *Sunday Sybarite* was good for New York business. But I think he savoured those hits for personal reasons. He hadn't made it in Manhattan until the cynics in the snugs of Dublin knew he had made it in Manhattan. I could understand that. I could understand that so well that it made John Paul's detached attitude seem inhuman: he hadn't just left Dublin, he had liquidated it.

But at least the e-mail was something, his first communication with anybody connected with the family in two years. I'd tried to get a correspondence going, based on that spark of contact, but no further communications came out of the internet ether.

Now, six months later, burdened with my new brief, I tried again:

To: JP@Wingatechevy.com
From : P_Dagg@hibernia.ie
Subject: On Tour

Dear John Paul
How's life in Texas? (Are you actually working at your father-in-law's dealership?)
    In Dublin there's more money than sense these days, and so the

courts are humming. Even caution horses like myself – remember that name? – are getting plenty of work.

Anyway, this summer I'm going to be taking a break from it all. I'm planning on travelling around the States for a few weeks, starting in New York. I've heard great things about Maverick from people who went to your wedding.

So basically I was hoping I could come down and see you for a few days. Would you be around in early August?

Sincerely
Peter D.

To my surprise, a reply came the very next day:

Dear Peter
Did my sister put you up to this?

JP

Well, what could I say in response? He had, as we used to say in school, sussed me out. He was no fool, John Paul Mountain, at least not in the ordinary sense of the word.

I don't believe, as my mother taught me, that honesty is necessarily the best policy, but in this instance, clearly, there could be no more BS, at least not of the unrefined variety. That night I drafted, and redrafted, this e-mail:

To: JP@Wingatechevy.com
From: P_Dagg@hibernia.ie
Subject: Motives

Dear John Paul,
Yes, it's true, Suzette put me up to this, but there's more to it than that. I really do want to see you myself – it's been, what,

24

four years since I turned around from that painting with all the squiggles in the Jeu de Paume and saw you standing there with that wry smile?

Do you know that when I was back in Paris the following summer I saw your mother? It was very shortly before she passed away, in fact. I've sometimes wondered if you ever got the letter of condolence I wrote to you soon afterwards. Perhaps I made a mistake in sending it to St Cloud, what with it being on the market, etc. Was it ever forwarded to you? Did you ever receive it? (A pity we didn't have e-mail addresses back then; the internet was surely invented for we wandering Irish!)

In any case, I'll say here now what I said in that letter. I know how much Nessa meant to you. I often heard it said around Dublin that you were more like brother and sister than mother and son. She was unique, irreplaceable, I know. If I ever get a chance, I'd like to talk to you about what she meant to me too.

Sincerely,
Peter

I didn't want to play the mother card, not yet at any rate, but I couldn't think of anything else that was likely to hook him. If I could bring his mother's tempting ghost, then John Paul would allow me to come. This was my theory.

At that time I was living a mile away, and a mile too far, from Suzette in a cosy little cell of an apartment in Ballsbridge. Every day before breakfast I would check my e-mail, about the time his Texan day, I imagined, was ending. For almost a week, nothing. Then at six o' clock one morning, there finally in my in-box was his reply, minutes old:

To: P_Dagg@hibernia.ie

From: JP87@lonestar.com
Subject: Come on over

Dear Peter
Kristen and I would delighted to see you. Early August, you say?
Fine. We'll be in town until the end of the month.

Until then,
John Paul

The invitation was not the only breakthrough; I took the use of his home e-mail address as a sign of trust, and an indication of just how paranoid he had been up to this point about Irish 'intervention'. I wrote back asking, pro forma, for the names of some good hotels. This time I didn't have to wait a week for his reply:

Don't be ridiculous, Peter. You're staying at our place, our new place. I'll pick you up at the airport. I am so looking forward to this, now.

I left Dublin Airport on 3 August. There to see me off were Suzette and Jerry. He was looking well that morning, better, dare I say it, than he had a right to. Jerry Mountain was, if nothing else, a survivor. It was the one career he'd stuck with for a lifetime.

To see Jerry at an airport was a rare sight indeed. Almost family now, I had been let in on his most shameful secret. Not even the *Sunday Sybarite* had found out that Jerry Mountain was afraid to fly. The last time he'd tried, years ago on the government jet going to Brussels, he'd thrown up on take-off all over the Minister of Agriculture.

How he got the money for that dapper summer suit (Kildare Bros., of course; nothing else would do) I don't know; perhaps he was still tapping into some of those fabled offshore funds. I liked the story, apocryphal though it probably was, of the taxpayer who grabbed Jerry's sleeve in the Europe Bar one night and said, 'That's my money you're wearing, Mister.'

Here was a man who wasn't going to be contributing a penny to the cost of his daughter's wedding. We hadn't even bothered to ask him. If we had, he would have just gone into his *I'm ruined – they ruined me* routine, and then resented us for making him expend that much energy. He was, as he reminded people in emergencies, a sick man.

Suzette's tears I expected – her gratitude for me having got this far with her brother was such that she would have, if it had been in her power, married me ten times over already. We'd come shockingly close to having sex. But her father's tears, tentative as they were, I was taken aback by. Jerry took hold of my hand, his grip both crushing and tremulous.

'Tell him to stop acting like this. Tell him there's plenty of time for hate later, Peter. We'll be dead long enough.'

I didn't know what to say. I just nodded, economically. Perhaps it was only at that moment I fully understood what I'd got myself into. Yes, I had agreed to be an ambassador, but for somebody else's country.

Suzette accompanied me to the very threshold of the boarding card checkpoint. Squeezing my hand she said, 'You don't know what this means to me, Peter. You don't know what this means.'

Oh but I did, for the look in her eye told me. I had not seen a stare of love like that since childhood. It moved me, to be sure – our final embrace was quite a scene – but, at the same time, it was a relief to get out of its range and into duty free.

Technically, I did spend some time travelling around the States before flying down to Maverick: three days in New York staying in the Chelsea apartment of an old friend of mine from Law.

The evening I arrived I went down to the East Village to meet Luke Fortune at Bunny Farrell's. A Tuesday night and the place was packed. Most of the clientele, as far as I could make out, were Manhattanites and European trust-fund kids. I wondered what the memorabilia all around the bar relating to Irish television programmes of the seventies and eighties – *Wanderley Wagon, The Live Mike, Hall's Pictorial Weekly* – could possibly mean to them. For me it was vaguely moving and slightly annoying to be reminded of the buried trivia of my childhood.

The Mountains were there, of course. Between a vintage Pacman and a primitive Space Invaders, Luke had created a grotto dedicated to *The Late, Late Show*. A series of framed black-and-white photographs traced the fall and rise of Gay Byrne's sideburns during the show's golden age. Right in the middle was a picture – dating from the early Seventies, judging from the barometer of Gay's grooming – with a young, shockingly vigorous Jerry Mountain in the hot seat. Dressed in a pin-stripe suit set off by a chunky, patterned tie, the longish hair slicked back, his own sideburns blazing, he looked like a fashion-conscious London gangster. The impassioned gesticulating hands added a touch of Mussolini. As a child, any time Jerry Mountain came on the television, I was sent to bed: he was the s-e-x man.

I had to search the memorabilia harder for any token of Nessa's RTE career. Finally I found a humble mortar-and-pestle, sitting on a small table in the corner of the smoky pool room; the pestle was chipped. Beside it a typed label read *Cooking with Nessa, 1965–1970*. That sad display made her heyday, her flourish, seem as dead and remote as that of the pre-historic Beaker People.

As Jerry Mountain began to appear on television, his wife began to disappear. In 1969 she sacrificed her sweetheart status by taking part in a highly publicised condom run on the Dublin-Belfast train; that may, in part, explain why John Paul and Suzette were products of the early Seventies. Even the birth of those telegenic children couldn't recapture Nessa's pristine image. Pleading the demands of motherhood, Nessa gave up her programme, though Jerry would later insist that the station had been on the verge of dropping it anyway.

Meanwhile, thanks in part to his media visibility, Jerry was developing a delicate web of business interests. He was on the board here, on the bandwagon there. By 1973, the Mountains could afford the Cloud House.

In the Eighties he went into politics. There was a new party to join, and Jerry loved to join a happening party. The Serious Radicals were as shiny and untried as the man himself. After a spell as a senator – anyone in Ireland can get elected senator – Jerry stood for the Dáil. He topped the poll in our constituency, that first time. But like any new Irish political party destined to sweep to power, the Dinner Party ended up in coalition.

Into the Nineties Jerry Mountain and the sleek political machine he had helped build were still forces to be reckoned with, but power was seeping out of both. The beginning of the end came late one night when the Gardaí stopped a car crawling around Fitzwilliam Square, one of Dublin's nodes of vice. Inside was the Serious Radicals' entire surviving parliamentary party.

Jerry Mountain, the least drunk of the four, was in dubious command of the Saab. To avoid breathalysation, or even worse trouble, he invoked an obscure privilege from the dangerous days after the civil war whereby TD's could not be detained if they were on their way to Leinster House for a vote. The Serious Radicals were in unanimity that they were on their way to Leinster House for a vote; they had simply got lost going around Fitzwilliam Square, again and again.

The Guards had no choice but to let the Dinner Party go, but, oddly enough, the *Sunday Sybarite* got wind of the story and, although it exaggerated the compromising position Jerry had been found in, the paper did establish one incontrovertible fact: that night the Dáil had adjourned at 7:15.

But if Jerry was in crisis, Nessa was a crisis.

After the children had started Montessori, she tried to rekindle her television career. But at Donnybrook she now had competition. RTE had a new cuisine diva, Emer Foyle, and Emer wouldn't budge from the kitchen set up in Studio 3. Nessa had to make do with the odd cookery spot on the *Late, Late*, many of whose viewers now saw her as Jerry Mountain's wife, not a personality in her own right.

She turned back to journalism, this time as a food critic rather than creator. The *Sunday Sybarite* offered her a column and, at first, 'A Lady at Lunch' set a new standard for erudite and scrupulous culinary criticism. However, as the eighties wore on, Nessa's reviews became increasingly aggressive. Twice Maurice Swarbrigg (successfully) defended the *Syb* in libel actions brought by ruined restaurateurs. The consensus around Dublin was that Nessa Mountain was not only a Lady who Lunched but also a Lady who Drank at Lunch, or even a Lady who was Drunk by Lunch. It didn't help that, by the turn of the decade, Nessa's reviews frequently failed to appear at all, her column written by a blander critic. Underneath each of those ersatz reviews a soon-famous editorial note appeared: *Nessa Mountain is recovering from food poisoning*. Eventually the *Syb* had enough of her unsteady copy and cancelled the column. Months later they broke the story about her husband's misadventures in Fitzwilliam Square. Nessa decided that she'd poisoned herself for too long. She left drink, Jerry, and Dublin behind, and started a new life in Paris.

It lasted eleven months.

'Where did you get all this stuff?' I asked Luke, as we sat together at the bar. He was standing me the first of several excellent pints of Guinness.

Luke shrugged the shoulders of his expensive crumply black suit. 'Contacts,' he said, as if I'd complemented him on the quality of a line of cocaine. 'Some people pissed that Donnybrook didn't renew their contracts as continuity announcers.' With a sigh he changed the subject. 'So you're going down to Texas to see Mr Mountain.'

I nodded. 'I am. And I'm not quite sure what to expect.'

Luke's forehead wrinkled. 'You're a brave man, Peter.'

'What do you mean?'

'He was up here in April for a week.'

'And?'

'Out of control. Had to bar him in the end, my own mate. But he did try to steal the original *Zig and Zag*.'

'That bad?'

I tried to make light of it, but Luke was not amused:

'As obnoxious as his father and as drunk as his mother.'

I'd heard enough of that kind of talk about the Mountains in Dublin, but I cooled my irritation with a long sip of Guinness.

'Do you think he's ready to come home?'

Luke shook his head. 'I don't know, and to tell you the truth I don't care. I've had enough of that family, or what's left of—'

For the first time ever, I saw Luke Fortune blush. He had forgotten that I was marrying into 'that family', what was left of it. Turning sharply, he shouted, 'Barry, same again for Peter!'

Part Two

TEXAS

From the air the city of Maverick was much greener than I expected. Don't get me wrong, I didn't think that Texas was going to be one big desert, or that Maverick was going to be a tumbleweed town, but it did look surprisingly lush down there, beneath the boundless royal-blue sky. I say city, but to my Irish eyes it was all one continuous woody suburb, dotted with glass boxes. When the plane banked I did glimpse a trim cluster of skyscrapers, but we landed so far away it might as well have been another city's downtown.

After such a long flight, I found it odd not to have to go through passport control or customs once I'd collected my luggage; even an unshaven nod from a sleepy official would have given me a greater sense of arrival, not that there were any unshaven, sleepy officials to be seen at Maverick Global Airport; they were uniformly presentable. Feeling as if I'd forgotten something, I proceeded unimpeded through to the tamely postmodern arrivals hall.

Though I knew I wouldn't see him, I was on the lookout for a man in black. Even after college, when it began to go out of style, the anti-colour remained the mainstay of his wardrobe, although the clothes themselves became strictly designer; it was John Paul's way of coping with the family's financial embarrassment: his affluence became pure show. The rumour was that he wore nothing but black silk boxers by Calvin Klein.

I recognised him only because he was one of the few people in the rendezvous area who was not a chauffeur with a little passenger name sign. Were those teeth, white as cold milk, the ones he'd left Ireland with? He looked heavier, healthier. But it was the clothes that got me, his sun-belt get-up: scuffless white runners, their soles platforms of foam; knee-length blue shorts, an unapologetic check pattern; a blue tee-shirt featuring a red exploding logo for the Maverick Brands (football? basketball? baseball?); and a cap advertising Abercrombie and Fitch, a firm that up to now I thought made clothes only for elderly Protestant ladies.

'Welcome to Maverick,' John Paul beamed, removing a pair of impenetrable wrap-around shades. It was himself, after a fashion.

'It's good to be here,' I replied, wondering if it was good to be here.

His smile rippled. 'How's the Caution Horse?'

'Oh, plodding along,' I replied, noting how his handshake came from the same mould as his father's.

Smooth as a thief, John Paul lifted the larger of my two bags as if he were stealing it. 'I'll take care of that, Peter.'

As we walked through the cool emptiness of the arrivals hall, he turned to me and said, 'So how's my sister, your intended?'

'Fine, just fine,' I replied slowly, wondering if breaking the taboo about his family so quickly, so casually was some attempt at reverse psychology. Had he asked there and then about Jerry I would have considered getting back on the New York plane.

I'd got a taste of Maverick's climate walking down the air bridge fifteen minutes before, but it was still a shock to step outside the terminal. Had there been a nuclear accident in the neighbourhood? And I had thought that in my light shirt and baggy khakis – casual, by my standards – I was dressed for the weather. My glasses fogged up instantly. My body took a heat bath.

'Wait a second,' I said, putting down my carry-on and taking out my handkerchief. 'Not used to this humidity.'

'Yep,' John Paul mused, 'it's getting to be summer round here.'

* * *

36

His car, too, was a shock. It wasn't a car. The moulds on the rear door identified it as a Blazer from Wingate Chevy, but to me it looked like a bright red tank with a black battering ram.

I said, 'You know, they've banned those cattle guards back home.'

John Paul snorted. 'Socialists.'

A loud bumper sticker read, *I wasn't born in Texas but I got here as soon as I could.*

He pointed a tiny remote control at the Blazer; it responded with a clipped shriek.

As John Paul loaded up my luggage – he insisted – I asked, 'When did you learn how to drive?'

'Day I got here.'

I was politely impressed for a moment, then said, 'Still, I didn't imagine one of these jeeps would be quite your thing.'

'You mean Sports Utility Vehicles, sport.' He brought down the rear door forcefully, then gave me a crafty glance. 'You thought I'd be more of a second-hand BMW man?'

Touché – I smiled. That was the car I'd bought a few months ago, with the first spoils of Irish divorce. I modified the subject. 'I guess you have to be an advertisement for the family business.'

'Utes are the future,' he replied.

'Utes?'

He nodded. 'Utes.'

'What about the poor old car?'

He shrugged, a touch wistfully. 'They'll be driven by the poor.'

'The poor will be driving BMWs?'

The question delighted him. 'No, no, no. That's an example of an *honorary* SUV. Shall we hit the road?'

Some road we hit. The Sam Maverick Tollway. It made the autobahn look like an overgrown boreen. When John Paul actually sped up as we approached the first row of toll booths

I braced myself for impact with a barrier, but we flashed through unimpeded.

'How come you get away without paying, John Paul?'

He smiled. 'I'm special.' He shot a finger at his windscreen. 'Plus I have an xpres-tag.'

I craned my neck. He was talking about a little white box by his rear-view mirror. 'Ingenious.'

He shrugged. 'Elementary.'

He turned on the radio. Country music oozed out. Surely this was John Paul's idea of an ice-breaking joke. I had an aversion to country and western – the sound of a slide guitar was enough to set my teeth on edge – and I presumed he did too. In Berchmans he'd been an aficionado of American proto-punk and German industrial music. After Trinity he formed his Doors rip-off band, the short-lived Erotic Politicians. Later I heard that he would listen to nothing but Gregorian chant.

I turned to him, but he just looked straight ahead, those Bono shades back in place.

A woman was singing slurpily about a multiple orgasm, though the subject was lightly veiled by an extended metaphor concerning bad weather – hurricanes, tornadoes, flash floods. At the end of the song there was a gushing station identification: we were tuned to HipCountry 102. Then the DJ said it was time once again for Roadkill Traffic with Gloria Muse. At auctioneer speed, she recited a catalogue of mishaps, of 'accidents working':

'Walter Cronkite expressway outbound at Merchant, lost load of glass across three lanes, slows to the Emporia; East Belt southbound at the thirty-five interchange, fatality-accident in the clearing stages; CenTex freeway North inbound at Tremain, car-be-cue and grass fire, slows to Aerodrome; Barbara Bush Boulevard at the Evans Parkway overpass, too-tall eighteen-wheeler – find alternate routes; Grigsby Drive between Hope and Leeds – closed due to police action; finally, I-29 the Splendora freeway inbound just past

Creekbend, injury-accident blocking the right two lanes, trapped passengers – Sky Angel en route – slows all the way to Hickory Farm Road.'

Gloria Muse hit the last syllable just as the punchy background music – closer to punk than country – came to an end. The basso-profundo DJ thanked her most sincerely for her performance.

'Shit,' was John Paul's reaction.

'Why?'

'Once we get off the tollway we have to take I-29 home – just where that accident is working.'

'You can't take back roads?'

'Surface roads?' His lips stiffened, as if he were editing out a tart commentary on the newcomer's naïveté. I might as well have suggested driving on water. 'No,' he added gently.

The longer we drove on the tollway, the more seriously I took John Paul's prediction about the Decline of the Car. For every normal vehicle there were two or three of his utes or ute-sized trucks. Their glinting names – Land Cruisers, Pathfinders, F150s – seemed more at home in the Gulf War than on the Gulf Coast. A GMC truck had been outfitted with a tiara of headlights and an obese set of tyres. It towered over the Blazer as we towered over the average car.

'I don't suppose there's any limit on how big these things can be,' I said.

'No,' he replied, sounding genuinely puzzled. 'Why should there?'

Soon after we'd flashed through another narrow toll booth – big vehicles and car underdogs jockeying and sidling for position until the lane system was re-established – the tollway, like a mature river, began to bend slowly, grandly to the south. The furniture warehouses and storage facilities and tyre outlets across the feeder road, as John Paul would teach me to say, gave way to mirrored boxes that housed energy companies. Land with nothing more than long grass and thin trees grew into forest with hints of suburbia.

Several leafy miles away stood downtown, a smart set of liquid skyscrapers. Much closer was another glass tower, an isolated giant, its upper reaches reminiscent of the sacrificial table of an Aztec temple. John Paul jabbed a finger at it and said, enunciating proudly, 'The Consort Tower.'

'Quite something.'

John Paul added a sly non-sequitur. 'By the way, Peter, I know why you're here.'

After a moment of self-consultation, I replied, 'Why am I here, John Paul?'

'You're Suzette's messenger.'

I kept things amiable. 'Oh really? Well, I did pay for my own ticket out here.'

'Ah, I see my father's hand at work.'

I laughed. 'And what do you do with messengers, John Paul, shoot them?'

He smiled. 'Oh no. I send them back as my messengers.' He flicked on his indicator. 'Time to leave the tollway.'

It took John Paul less than thirty seconds to cruise across four lanes, angling into risky gaps as if they'd been reserved for him. We made the nearer turn-off lane yards before the thick white line that separated it from the ongoing tollway. Even so, a small, rusty pick-up truck sailed in front of us, missing the barrier of yellow barrels by a few feet. John Paul didn't seem to notice.

'You drive like a native.'

'I wasn't born in Texas but I got here as fast as I could.'

On the sharply curving overpass he edged past the pick-up.

The sun had become larger and much lower than when we'd last faced west, not ten minutes before. I pulled down the shade and put on my clip-ons, but the light was still intense. John Paul noticed my discomfort.

'Don't worry, sunset's a quick business here.'

'Good.'

'Not that it's going to be much cooler.'

'Wouldn't notice it in here.'

This was a hint that the SUV's air-conditioning had become a little too intense. John Paul didn't take it. Instead he said:

'You won't notice the heat anywhere once you're inside. Did you know Maverick is the atmospheric ceiling capital of the world?'

I listened for irony; I heard none. 'I had no idea,' I replied.

'Air-conditioning is an art form here. They're getting better and better at hiding it. In our house you're cool and you don't even realise why.'

By now John Paul had merged with the dense traffic on the freeway and established himself in the far lane. We crawled forward, lording it over the cars that crawled around us; we'd left the economic selection of the tollway behind. The freeway was a free-for-all. It soon grew tedious. HipCountry 102 was playing 'the brand new one' from Trey Dasher, 'The Good Lord's Dating Service'. At this rate, we were going to hear the station's entire playlist. What this city needed was a few Bombardier buses.

For a time the conversation became as slow as the traffic. To take my mind off the music, I studied the scenery, studied it so closely that if it hadn't been for the harsh evidence of the sun sinking ahead of us I would have sworn we were going around in circles. On either side of the freeway the same busy strip of commerce – fast food, slower food, gas stations, bright shopping centres – seemed to repeat itself, like the backdrop of a cartoon chase. Looking ahead all I could see was a chaos of signs.

The only places that stood out were the new suburbs pictured on broad billboards: Secret Colony; Hampton Estates; Walden Lake (Preferred North Shore); Tiverton Village at Historic Johnson Landing – A Gated Community. Gated community: I wondered if that counted as an oxymoron.

The visuals were heavy on cool sunsets, lone golfers, blond

children frolicking in pervert-free forests. *Take Pecan 2 Miles West from Highway 9*, read the directions for Serenity Crescent. *From the 120s to the 350s*. I did a quick calculation, dollars to punts. For the upper range of that money Suzette and I had just scraped together the down-payment on a Victorian labourer's cottage in need of fundamental repairs.

I asked John Paul, 'Have you ever seen any of these colonies or clubs or historic landings?'

'Absolutely. We must have visited every master-planned community west of Maverick before settling on New Plantation.'

'You live in one of these places?'

'You seem surprised.'

'Well, not exactly. It's just that . . . last time I met you, you were living with a heroin dealer on rue Mouffetard. Not to mention you growing up in the Cloud House.'

'Indeed, not to mention me growing up at St Cloud.' He pronounced it the proper way, the French way.

'New Plantation. I suppose Kristen feels comfortable in that kind of world.'

'Oh, no,' John Paul retorted, taking his hidden eyes off the road and looking over at me, 'she wanted to buy a place in the University District. The master-planned community was my idea.'

'I see,' I said, secretly astonished.

We began to pass patches of undeveloped land, then long stretches of scrubby country. In the distance I could see the yellow skeletons of half-completed houses.

'Is that a master-planned community going up over there?'

John Paul snorted. 'They wish. That's just a ratty subdivision.'

On an overpass we could finally see the I-29 inbound injury-accident that had been advertised, twice more at this stage, on Roadkill Traffic. Or rather, we could see the big production it had become. The trapped passengers had been liberated and removed from the scene, leaving behind a train of at least six tow-trucks on the hard shoulder – their yellow lights flashing fussily in the blood-red sunlight – bookended by police cars, one blue, one white. Just behind the lead police car was a grey old boat from the seventies. When the Blazer eventually filed by the dead car, I could see just how bad the damage was: the whole rear end had all but fallen off.

'Rubbernecker,' John Paul growled at me.

'Excuse me?'

He imitated my flexible fascination. I wished he would keep his eyes on the road.

'Ah,' I said, leaning back in my seat. 'Have they towed away the other vehicle already?'

'No way. Must have been a hit and run. Undoubtedly a ute.'

'Undoubtedly.'

Once past the lead police car we picked up speed quickly – the spectator sport, rubbernecking, had been the only thing slowing us down.

'See that flag up ahead?' John Paul asked.

I could. In the distance, at least a mile away on our side of the freeway, I could make out a blur of red stripes. 'Are we coming to an airbase or something?'

'No,' John Paul laughed, not unkindly. 'That's the dealership.'

Just before it was another billboard, this one featuring not a master-planned community but a beefy smiling man with a broad moustache – BOB WINGATE – 'MR DISCOUNT'.

'Peter, I'd like you to meet my father-in-law.'

'Delighted. Mr Discount, hey?'

'Suburban Bob to his friends.'

'Will I have the pleasure of meeting him?'

'Absolutely. We have the grand tour set up for tomorrow, when Kristen's working.'

I wanted to ask him whether he worked there, and if so how much – wanted to know what John Paul Mountain was actually doing with his life in Maverick, Texas. But now was not the time, not even remotely the right time. We were under the skyscraping flag's sway.

'Big flag,' I said.

'Second biggest in the city,' John Paul volleyed back.

'Where's the largest one?'

'McLaurin Ford on the East Side.'

'You sound a little jealous.'

He shrugged. 'Big competitive thing among the dealerships.'

'For purely patriotic reasons, I'm sure.'

'You got it.'

This dealership looked like the campus of a shiny new university. The main building, with its façade of glass and white square pillars, set the architectural tone; even the box marked 'Program Cars' looked as if it housed advanced scientific research. The arty banners, distinguishing trucks from cars, might have been for special exhibitions. The fields of vehicles were dominated by SUVs – this was the student body of the future.

'What's it like marrying into a family business?' I asked.

'What's it like marrying into a family?' he asked back.

We passed a whole slew of other dealerships, all of them lesser institutions. A few miles further on I thought we were approaching a franchise that might rival the Wingates' family business in size and style – the vehicles looked shiny enough – but on closer inspection it turned out to be the vast packed car park of a shopping centre. With its ochre façade and quaint conical turrets it looked like an elongated Tuscan villa.

'Rustic Mall,' John Paul explained. 'Until they get Town Square finished at New Plantation, those are our local stores.'

A green freeway sign said, *New Plantation Blvd Next 2 Exits*. As he crossed the lanes John Paul didn't put on his signal; on the exit slope he didn't reduce his speed; so I was relieved when, on the feeder road, he chose to obey a red light and we came to a refreshing stop. He turned under the freeway – the groan of the traffic above briefly muffling out a country song comparing past boyfriends to past presidents – sped up again when provoked by a yellow, and crossed the other side of the feeder road onto the boulevard. It was divided by a broad grassy strip and overhung by the writhing limbs of mature trees. Foggy sunlight lay in our path.

'I've never seen those kind of trees before. They're quite lovely.'

'Southern live oaks. They were part of the original plantation.'

'So there's something in the name.'

'Something.'

'What did they plant?'

'Cotton. No – sugar.'

'Who did the planting?'

He glanced at me. 'You mean, were there slaves?'

'Yes.'

'I believe there were, at one point. There's a museum if you're really interested.'

'A museum?'

'Yeah, in the Welcome Center.'

'Fair enough.'

John Paul smiled. 'This is America, Peter. They don't try to hide their history.'

Something you could learn from, I silently replied.

After about a mile, the woods ended and we reached a junction. On the other side, planted in the grass strip, was a brick-fringed slab of dark green marble, inscribed with community's name, the letters done in gold leaf. On either side of the road stood a red-brick landmark – a folly, we would call it in Ireland – topped off by a lantern and a weathervane, pointing westward.

'Welcome to New Plantation,' John Paul said, as he gunned forward from the stop sign.

'I see you're not a gated community.'

He shook his head. 'No need for gates. We're beyond crime here.'

45

*   *   *

Inside the community proper, traffic was idyllically light. Then again, there were only so many homes to go to. For a few hundred yards, behind lines of young trees and landscaped trails, we cruised by finished red-brick houses, but soon the scene was one of vast incompleteness: bright yellow frames padded with material that advertised itself as Dubchek Home Wrap; foundation slabs sprouting the pipes of imminent buildings.

'When will this place be finished?'

'Oh, not for another ten years at least.'

'Ten years?'

'At least. You've got to realise we have twenty-one square miles out here. Go another mile down the boulevard and it turns into a dirt track.'

'How many houses are they planning on building?'

'Fifteen thousand is a figure I've heard. And the other New Plantations are going to be even bigger.'

'The *other* New Plantations?'

John Paul nodded. 'One for every side of the city.'

We came to a crossroads. To our right was a crudely miniaturised mansion, its white pillars too fat for its scale, its porch too deep. On the roof was the same lantern and weathervane I had seen on the sentry structures. This was the Welcome Center. A sign pointing to our left said, *Plymouth Village North*. John Paul turned that direction, the Blazer rocking as he did so.

At the end of another block of building sites, we reached seasoned granite walls and drove through urn-crowned gateless gateposts. Inside was an enclave of cul-de-sacs, detached houses, and flawless lawns.

The Mountain-Wingates lived on Pocahontas Lane. No two houses were quite the same, nor were they much different. John Paul turned into the driveway of one of the smaller ones, which was nevertheless still larger than Maurice Swarbrigg's trophy house in

Dublin 4. Its busy red-brick façade featured gables, columns, arches, even an ox-eye window. John Paul pressed a remote clipped to his sunshade and one of the twin garage doors began to rise smoothly; John Paul had the front of the Blazer inside before it was fully up. In the other space was a metallic green sports car. I turned to John Paul.

'Honorary SUV?'

'Yes indeed,' he replied, switching off the ignition. 'My dear wife's Camero. Limited edition.'

'Is that so?'

He took off his shades. 'Kristen likes rarities.'

In the dim automatic light his eyes looked tired.

'I'd like to meet her,' I replied.

Even the garage was air-conditioned. John Paul brought me and my suitcase through a side door and a laundry room where an industrial-sized washer and dryer were booming away. Through another door and into another atmosphere again. We put my luggage down on the darkly polished hardwood floor of a large hall. Down into it swept a broad staircase. At the top was a bridge that also overlooked a spacious living room. Leaning on the balustrade, one foot crossed over the other precisely, like a ballet dancer, was a skinny young woman with straw-blonde hair. She was wearing a white cotton top and ankle-revealing jeans.

'Hi there, Peter,' she said in a sweet, slightly hoarse voice.

'Kristen, hello,' I replied.

'JP, I'll be right down. Make Peter comfortable in the living room.'

'OK,' John Paul replied, cheerfully obedient. 'Peter, we'll leave your bags here for now.'

In the high-ceilinged living room I felt Kristen's presence before she even entered. It was tastefully furnished, accented with eclectic artefacts and antiques, a striking contrast to the mere confusion of the house's exterior. Inside, a controlling intelligence had been at work, a mind with firm aesthetic opinions. Even the coffee-table books looked deep. Normally, I'm not a great fan of abstract art, but the unframed triptych above the long fireplace, suggesting desert flowers, was something that I could live with myself. Nessa Mountain would have been proud.

I sat down on a slim couch that was more comfortable than it looked.

'Iced tea?' John Paul asked.

'Yes, please.'

'Not something stronger?' He made it sound like a test.

'No, iced tea will be fine.'

'Peach-passionfruit or mango-raspberry?'

I smiled. 'Whatever you're having yourself, John Paul.'

He nodded, waiterly. 'Mango-raspberry it is then.'

John Paul disappeared; Kristen appeared; I stood up again. Her handshake was so light that I felt I'd rather crushed her knuckles in response. Now I could see the details I had missed, looking up in the hall: the butterfly clips that held up her hair, the subtle sprinkle of freckles on her face, the embroidery on her top. But above all, the eyes that I'd taken to be green were blue up close.

I had seen one photograph and one photograph only of John Paul's wedding – Iremonger is not the most reliable archivist – and it had not done her justice. My fiancée came immediately to mind. Suzette had a most photogenic face (she did some modelling in her late teens), but in person she was more problematic. Over the years, John Paul had dated some beautiful girls, more conventionally beautiful, certainly, than Kristen Wingate, but then again, Kristen wasn't a girl; she was a woman – distinct, distinctive. Suddenly, John Paul's wedding, that remote, almost abstract event, was very real.

'It's so good to have you here, Peter.'

Her accent was no more pronounced than her husband's. Meeting her elsewhere I would have known straightaway she was an American, but not a Texan.

'Thanks for inviting me.'

'Oh, not at all. We've been really excited about you coming. My parents, too. They can't wait to meet you. They really loved the Irish people who made it out for the wedding. Do you know you're the first person from Dublin to come out and stay with us?'

'I assumed that, yes.'

We sat down on opposite ends of the slim couch. How could I begin to deal with all the revisionism, well-meaning though it was, in her little welcoming speech? The Irish people who made it out – as if it had been bad weather that had prevented Jerry and Suzette from attending the wedding.

I would deal with it by going along with it, of course. I wasn't here to question the polite fictions that been built up around the raw history of John Paul's family. I was here to bring him home.

John Paul came back in with three glasses of iced tea on a tray.

'Bonding with my wife?'

'Surely,' I replied, taking my drink. It was delicious. I had to check myself from drinking all of it in one go. They were both watching me. 'Didn't realise I was so thirsty,' I said.

'Better get used to it,' John Paul said.

Kristen gave him a brief, sharp look, then turned to me. 'When you're done with that, Peter, how about the grand tour?'

'Sounds good.'

Soon my glass was empty.

While John Paul brought my suitcase upstairs, Kristen showed me the rest of the downstairs: the kitchen with its turquoise marble counter tops and army of utensils; the vast en-suite master bedroom, complete with matching his-and-her bathroom counters; the surprisingly intimate dining room; and, in every nook and cranny, another half-bathroom, as if the house had been designed for the chronically incontinent. Why did they need an upstairs?

John Paul showed me why. When I reached the landing, he marched me across the bridge, through a lounging area dotted with geometrically patterned glazed pottery, and into a large bedroom. It overlooked the Mountain-Wingates' relatively modest back garden and the giant, velvety green of a golf course. I put my carry-on down on the four-poster bed and took a closer look at the view.

'You're looking down on the seventh hole, a par three. Trickier than it looks.'

'You play *golf* now, John Paul?'

He nodded seriously. 'Taking lessons from Drew Pagan, the new club professional. Used to play on the Canadian PGA.'

All I could say was, 'Where will this decadence end, John Paul – bridge?'

He shook his head. 'No. I'll be trying out for the polo team once the equestrian centre is open. Parker Nevle, our block captain, is going to set me up with a pretty reasonable pony.'

'Any danger of an overly ambitious tee-shot giving me a rude awakening?'

'No way. The customised glass is especially designed to withstand golf balls. Swiss invention. C'mon, let me show you what else we have up here.'

I was led through rooms for which there had been no equivalents even in the Cloud House – the games room, the aquarium, the meditation space. Finally we walked down a corridor, created by two more bathrooms, to the side of the house.

'That's Kristen's study,' he said, gesturing to the right. 'And this is mine,' he added, opening the door in front of us.

It was a bright, clinical room with no clutter on the large walnut desk that faced the window, not even a disk beside the Dell computer with a broad-faced monitor. In one corner was a green filing cabinet. There was a key inserted in the lock in the top corner, but the card slots on the drawers were empty. On one of the white walls hung a small framed ink drawing. Mildly curious, I walked towards it, until I made out its subject: Charlesfort, Kinsale, possibly the view the Mountains had from their summer home. How happy they'd been down there, as a family, was one of Suzette's favourite refrains. Early one morning the children found their parents, who had left them the night before with a baby-sitter and gone to a party in Oysterhaven, curled up together asleep in the long grass behind the house.

If John Paul caught me taking an interest in that little window on the past, he didn't let on. He went over to a wardrobe and slid back one of the mirrored doors. A few wire hangers swayed and touched. In a corner, underneath a deep shelf stacked with a motley collection of hats, was a small safe about three feet tall. It had a grey rippling metal façade.

John Paul knelt down and whispered, 'Come here,' as if he were showing me day-old puppies.

'What is it?'

'What does it look like? It's where we keep the guns.'

He started on the combination. I didn't want to know it.

'We, John Paul?'

'OK, where I keep the guns. My wife is disturbingly un-fond of firearms, for an American.'

The door opened smoothly. Despite myself, I crouched down beside him and peered inside. I could see two weapons, as well as various clips and accessories. One item looked like a silencer, but I wasn't positive. For all my legal experience, I had not participated in a single case involving firearms.

He put the first gun, a small stainless-steel revolver with a dotted wooden grip, in the palm of his hand and lifted it towards me. I backed away a little as if it had a bad odour.

'Smith and Weston .22,' he said.

'Pretty.' And it was.

'Only use I have for a compact.' He laughed; I twitched back a smile, suspecting that I'd missed the joke.

'Want to try it?' he asked.

'No thank you.'

'Guns make you anxious, Peter?'

'Oh, not at all. I've been watching them on television for years.'

'Well, maybe you're right to be concerned. You know what they say: If someone shows you a gun on the first day of your vacation, it's bound to go off on the last.'

I smiled grimly.

'You don't approve,' he said.

'Not entirely.'

'An armed society is a polite society,' he lectured brightly.

'You don't seriously believe that, John Paul, do you?'

'No, I don't seriously believe that.'

He winked and put the revolver back in its place and took out the other weapon, this one much bigger, a matte-black pistol. John Paul made a show of pointing it away from me.

'Now this is the baby I'd like to have sleeping beside me, except that my dear wife won't allow it.'

'Perhaps she's jealous. What's this one called?'

'Nine mil. Parabellum Sig 26, made by Sauer. German.'

'*Vorsprung durch technik*.'

'Exactly,' he replied, as if we saw eye to eye on the subject.

He put the precious weapon back and closed the safe door. 'I'm saving up for a Beretta,' he said as he scrambled the combination.

'Do you have to have any licence for these things?'

'Only if I carry one as a concealed weapon,' he said as we stood up.

'And do you?'

'Do I what? Have a licence or carry a concealed weapon?'

'Both.'

52

He tapped my shoulder. 'Let me put it this way, Peter. I believe the more licence you have, the less freedom you have.'

'You're pulling my leg again,' I concluded.

He didn't have a chance to either confirm or deny; his gun-controlling wife walked in. When she saw the open wardrobe door, Kristen gave her husband a smouldering stare. He slid it closed.

'John Paul was just showing me his stamp collection,' I said.

Kristen smirked. 'Well,' she said, 'are either of you philatelists hungry?'

'Oh, that's right, Peter, I haven't told you yet. We're bringing you out to dinner.'

'Have you ever had Tex-Mex?' Kristen asked me.

'Well, yes, there's this place in Dublin—'

'You've never had Tex-Mex,' said John Paul.

Kristen announced that she'd booked a table for eight-thirty and that we needed to leave in the next fifteen minutes. I told my hosts I'd freshen up quickly and meet them downstairs. In the guest room I took out my GreenGlobe calling card and used the phone on the bedside table. The female recorded voice that gave me warm instructions in soft Irish syllables left me more homesick than my fiancée's own sleepy tone.

'Hope I didn't wake you up, dear.' Phoning home meant phoning her mobile. Suzette never used the ordinary phone in the mews off Baggot Street she shared with two other media women.

'No,' Suzette replied, suddenly alert. 'Don't worry about that. Never worry about that. Are you there?'

'I'm here.'

'How is he?'

'Worse than we imagined.'

'Oh, Jesus. Doing coke again?'

'Worse. He's playing golf.'

'Peter, be serious.'

'I am being serious. You don't understand. He's bought into some notion of normality that only someone deeply disturbed could think of as being normal. He's not himself, Suzette. He's unrecognisable.'

'I'm sure I'd recognise him,' she said.

I thought, If you'd recognise him why don't you come out here and do the dirty work?

I said, 'Suz, all I'm saying is that I don't want to get your hopes up. This is going to be a tricky operation.'

'Peter,' she replied, the satellite transmitting her intensity all too well, 'you've got to tell him about Jerry. Tell him he doesn't have all the time in the world to sort himself out.'

'I know, dear,' I interrupted, 'we'll be dead long enough.'

As soon as I'd used her father's phrase I regretted it, but Suzette didn't seem to pay me much attention. 'Tell him this is more than a wedding,' she continued. 'Tell him this isn't just about him. It's about the Mountains.'

That, I calculated, was the last thing John Paul wanted to be told.

'I will tell him, Suzette,' I replied blandly, 'I'll tell him all of that. In good time. But you've got to let me go about things my way, love.'

'Ah yes, your way. Softly, softly.'

'Yes, softly, softly.'

Thanks to the quality of the GreenGlobe connection I heard my fiancée breathe anxiously and felt a whisper of guilt. 'Listen,' I said delicately, 'I have to go. They're bringing me out to dinner.'

'How kind of them.'

'It's somewhere very casual.'

'I'm sure you'll have a great time.'

'Suzette, I'll phone you when I have some news.'

'I hope you'll phone me news or no news.'

'Of course I will, dear.'

'What's the number there?'

'You want the number here?'

'Yes.'

'But what if he answers? What if she answers?'

'I think I can handle that, sweetie.'

'Of course, of course. You're right. Got a pen handy?'

She had. I dictated the number, turning the last digit from a five into a nine. Later I could insist that, in her excitement, she'd taken it down wrong.

For at least the fifth time the compact bronze-skinned man filled our water glasses with grave efficiency. The clots of ice crackled after he'd gone on to the next table. All through the meal I had been studying the way John Paul treated the staff of El Norte. My parents had once sat a few tables away from his parents and some of their braying cronies in the Lighthouse, Dublin's semi-legendary seafood restaurant.

My father recounted with horror how Jerry had snapped his fingers at the waiters and called them *garçon*. This was in the days when Jerry Mountain could snap his fingers and, no matter how much hatred they were stockpiling against him, the plain people of Ireland would be at his service. My mother was less bothered by Jerry's authoritarian antics than by Nessa Mountain's boozing. 'Drinking wine like water,' she said twice.

A decade later, in a very different kind of restaurant, their son was drinking green frozen sludge like water but treating the waiters, and the sub-waiters, reasonably. I felt uncomfortable when he casually referred to the iced-water man, who might have been fifty, as the 'busboy', but he did thank him each time he topped up his glass. With our waiter proper, Cy, he took on a positively egalitarian tone, bantering about tortilla chips and knives.

Here was Cy again: a boy's face, a bouncer's body.

'Ready for another round of 'ritas there, folks?'

'Not for me,' Kristen replied. While I had been on the phone to her sister-in-law, she had put on understated make-up that made me look again, and again, at her subtle beauty. But she was not completely at ease, as her husband appeared to be; there was some reserve in Kristen now that went beyond her status as our designated driver. Her blue eyes darted between John Paul and Cy as they debated the merits of various top-shelf tequilas. They reached a consensus about Presidente Blue; John Paul turned to me for acquiescence. I didn't want to give it that easily. First time round he had ordered my margarita without even consulting.

'The ordinary stuff is quite powerful enough for me,' I said. 'And no salt this time.'

Cy nodded his acceptance of the order, but John Paul responded with a fierce smile, 'Come on now, Peter, I don't want to hear any *quit* in your voice. We've got a longways to go.'

I replied, 'I'm with you all the way, John Paul.'

Cy promised to be back 'immediatamente' with the drinks. We went back to our heavy meal and leaner conversation. John Paul had done most of the talking, and most of the talking had been about the food. He took great delight in instructing me in the art of the fajita, encouraging me to pile on top of a warm, downy tortilla strips of chicken, strips of beef, shredded cheese, fat beans, yellow rice, and slather the melting mass with the red, white, and green – pico de gallo, cream cheese, and guacamole. When it came time for the all important tuck-and-fold, John Paul reached over and actually fingered my food. Kristen gave him a disapproving look; his hand retreated.

The restaurant was as crowded as our table-top. A score of black-aproned waiters circulated in a space big enough to house several executive jets. On the high walls, plaster had been artificially peeled away to reveal plump terracotta bricks. The heavy wooden fans that dropped from the corrugated metal ceiling were mere symbols of the herculean air-conditioning system keeping the place so vehemently cool.

The deep and deeply full car park had been my first indication of what a big production El Norte was going to be. (Up to that point John Paul and Kristen had given the impression that they were bringing me to a little neighbourhood restaurant.) John Paul happily resorted to valet parking. With the brio of a conquistador dismounting from his stallion, he swung up beside the velvet ropes and ceded the wheel of the Blazer to a crisply dressed Hispanic boy.

The building looked like a cross between a Docklands warehouse and a spaghetti western mission church. El Norte's had a green neon subtitle: UNDER TEX-MEX RULE. In the lobby at least two dozen people were waiting, many of them brandishing pagers on long perspex handles. We walked through the crowd to the hostess's lectern, John Paul leading the way.

'Doesn't seem quite fair,' I confided to Kristen, 'sauntering in like this.'

'If they wanted a table that badly,' she replied, 'they should have booked like us.' I didn't argue.

Cy was back. While he and John Paul swapped tough witticisms about the potency of the green stuff, I took the opportunity to ask Kristen about her family.

'I understand you have a brother and a sister.'

'That's right.'

'Still live here in Maverick?'

'No. Maverick isn't their sort of town. Megan is in Austin, Trace just moved to Portland.'

'What do they do?'

She sighed breezily. 'Meg is still running her eco-feminist camps and Trace is training to be a Zen chiropractor.'

'No chance either of them will come back and take over Wingate Chevy one day?'

She shook her head. 'No chance.'

'So that leaves you.'

She gave me a wry stare. 'That leaves me with a Ph.D. in Art History, eventually.'

John Paul was done with Cy. He looked at me and said, 'Not a lot of opportunities to talk about John Singer Sargent when you're trying to sell nicely equipped Suburbans.'

Time for a soft risk. 'So that leaves . . .'

'That leaves me,' John Paul said.

Did I see Kristen flinch? Certainly she said, 'Of course there's always Truck Nation.'

'Truck Nation?'

'Yes, they're the fastest growing large vehicle retailer in the country. Last year they bought up about thirty franchises.'

'The McDonald's of the industry,' John Paul grumbled.

'That's not going to be Dad's problem if he sells,' Kristen countered.

'If he sells.'

Time, I judged, to deflate the conversation. So I said to Kristen, 'Your brother was one of the grooms at the wedding, right?'

The frost that had formed around her melted away. She leaned forward earnestly.

'You haven't seen the pictures?'

John Paul started to manufacture another epic fajita.

I replied, 'Not a representative sample. Heard a great deal about it, of course.'

'Of course,' she said quietly, then brightened. 'But you must see the video. John Paul, we must show him the video.'

'Don't worry, he'll see it,' John Paul replied, tucking and rolling his tortilla.

'We sent everyone who came a copy of the tape,' Kristen told me.

I frowned. 'You see, Kristen, American tapes don't play on Irish VCRs.'

'Oh, we didn't think of that.'

'You can get them converted,' John Paul muttered, and devoured half the packed tortilla.

'In any case,' I said, 'I'd love to see it.'

She reached out and touched my sleeve while her husband chewed. 'It's such a pity you weren't able to make it over.'

John Paul smirked and choked softly.

I shrugged. 'It was difficult . . .'

Kristen nodded sadly, not paying any attention to her husband, who was now washing down his food with a long draught of margarita. 'I know,' she said.

Her husband came back into the conversation with a bang: 'But wait a second, did we even *invite* you, Peter?'

Kristen stared up at the wooden fans. I said, 'Well, yes, technically. That invitation for Suzette, the one that arrived at the last minute, it said Suzette and Guest. I was Suzette's guest at that stage. Her steady guest. So if she'd come I guess I would have come too.'

'But she didn't come,' John Paul said. That was satisfaction in his voice, not resentment.

Kristen smiled, looked at me, looked at him. 'It's never too late.'

John Paul looked around, located Cy tables away collapsing a tray stand – and clicked his fingers.

I studied Kristen, solemnly dipping the curlicue of a tortilla chip in green sauce. I could help her. Help her with her John Paul problem. (Didn't anyone who became involved with John Paul end up with a John Paul problem?) And she could help me. Kristen was the key.

The next morning, Saturday, she left for the dealership before I woke up. After breakfast John Paul and I walked along the artificial beach of New Plantation's artificial lake. The sand had so little give in it that it was more like sandpaper. The water was such a rich turquoise that I suspected it had been dyed. On the far shore the berths and the terrace of the mini-marina were almost empty. It was just after nine but felt like permanent midday. John Paul had given me a Maverick Steers baseball cap to shade my hangover but I was still suffering; that fourth margarita had been a tactical error, salt or no salt.

Bareheaded, John Paul looked considerably sharper, as if he'd been able to store away the damage. Maybe it was visible in his eyes but he'd worn his Bono shades even to the breakfast table. And I had been damaged in other ways. Leaving the restaurant last night I had been mugged by mosquitoes, but here, by the water, not a bite.

'This repellent you gave me is certainly doing the job.'

John Paul shook his head. 'It's more than the bug spray, friend. The first year I was in Maverick I was as much of a victim as you are, spray or no spray.'

'Must be our sweet Irish blood,' I said. John Paul simply continued:

'But then we took the tour out here. The control system here is second to none. It was one of the deciding factors for us in choosing this place over Dapplewood. By rights, down here we should be running into squadrons of skeeters.'

I laughed. 'In other words, they've kept the barbarians at the gate.'

John Paul didn't say anything. Instead he stopped, turned on his heels on the dense sand, and looked across the turquoise lake – no breeze, were those ripples artificially created too? – looked for such a long time that eventually I had to ask, 'Waiting for a ship to come in, John Paul?'

His tongue worked its way lumpily across the top teeth of his closed mouth. Then, as if he were raising a visor, he flipped up his shades onto his slicked-back hair.

'Peter?' There was mischief in his voice and in his glassy Nessa eyes.

'Yes?'

'How did Jerry convince you to come out here?'

It was too early for this kind of conflict. I didn't contradict him, directly. I said, 'You're sure it's your father behind all this?'

He gave me an arch don't-insult-my-intelligence look. I shrugged and nodded as if he were being reasonable. 'Suzette and I had . . . some conversations.'

'She's always been a daddy's girl,' he said, almost nostalgically, then added sharply, 'you want to watch that, Peter.'

I nodded meditatively. 'I will watch that, John Paul. Thank you. But tell me – and I hope you don't think me interfering for asking this – but do you ever see a time – in the distant future, of course – when you and your father can begin to . . . repair some of the damage that's been done to your relationship by all these' – the gesture I made looked like some failed conjuring trick – 'these . . . trials and tribulations?'

John Paul stared down at the water's edge, biting his lower lip, as if he were watching footage of his family's ugly history. He began to nod his head, vigorously. 'Yes,' he said, 'yes, I do.'

The next question I asked very delicately. 'And could I possibly help in some small way to bring this about?'

The visor came down. 'Yes, you could, Peter. You could start by bringing Nessa back to life.'

He strode off down the beach, but left no footprints behind.

No, I couldn't bring Nessa back to life, but I could keep in mind what she told me the last time I saw her.

Paris. Late June. I had just been called to the Bar and was rewarding myself with a short holiday in my favorite place. But I was not happy. Suzette and I were in the middle of a break-up – she was doing most of the breaking – the kind of break-up that either sets you on your separate paths for good, or drives you back together again with a vengeance.

Through the Irish grapevine – what a vigorous plant – Nessa heard I was in town. She left a message with the people I was staying with out in Neuilly inviting me to dinner. I knew what this was all about, or so I thought. Nessa wanted to play counsellor, re-matchmaker, in spite of her own marriage, or perhaps because of it.

I caught the RER to Les Halles, crossed a hazy Boulevard de Sebastopol, and soon found the rue des Saltimbanques, a serpentine street a few blocks from that giant toy the Pompidou Centre. Nessa had told me her apartment was directly across from a jewellery boutique. I saw it – Galerie Malakov – and went over to its glowing niche of a window. The place was open and I thought about buying one of the preciously displayed *bijoux* for Suzette. Thought about it, and thought against it, for now. I didn't want to be late for dinner. And I wasn't at all sure that Suzette Mountain was an investment I could afford any more.

Across the slim street I pressed the button beside the tag COLUMBUSIER/KELLY and was buzzed in almost immediately. She must have seen me, or been watching me, window-shopping. Up two flights of stairs Nessa was waiting at the nondescript entrance of her apartment. It turned out to be a long cool vault of exposed beams and granite walls quietly modernised with small abstract canvases. This may have been her boyfriend's apartment, but Nessa had most definitely made it her home. A tight spiral staircase led to who knew what on a second floor; she didn't give me the grand tour. But she was gracious and warm, giving me a vigorous kiss on both cheeks, making just the right amount of fuss over the chocolate truffles I'd brought, before putting them away.

The more Nessa Mountain drank, the more people in Dublin had talked about how beautiful she had been when she was young. Now in her not-so-early fifties, dressed in smart beige clothes, scarf artfully tied around her rather flushed neck, hair boldly bobbed, offering me something to drink with all the control of someone who won't be taking anything herself, she looked more handsome than beautiful. There was a slight mannish quality about her that I sometimes caught in her daughter's profile too. But she certainly looked better than she did towards the end of her Dublin and drinking days, though the evidence remained on her broad face, beneath the make-up, like the traces of ancient water channels on a dry planet.

'Where's Georges?' I asked.

Georges was the new man in Nessa's new life, a sixty-ish widower with grown-up children who did something significant for a merchant bank for which there was no exact correspondence in the Anglo-American financial world. I'd met him once only, with Suzette in Dublin, and she and I were not going to reconcile fast enough for me to see him again at the funeral – the tense Mass at St Eustache, the ugly scene at the Père Lachaise columbarium.

In the months before her death there was a lot of talk, much of it from Suzette, that Nessa and Georges would marry, now that her foreign divorce had come through. (Poor Nessa, if she'd lived a little longer she would have seen the constitutional ban she loathed finally disappear. Jerry's feelings on the matter were equally strong. It was one of the few things they could agree on in the terminal stage of their marriage. Both had played prominent roles in the first, disastrous divorce campaign back in the eighties, when they were still very publicly a power couple. It was as if they were trying to legislate their own breakdown.)

Georges? Georges was away on some arcane mission to a bank in Frankfurt. Nessa added:

'So I thought this would be an excellent opportunity for you and me to have a quiet little dinner together.'

'I'm delighted you asked me,' I replied, finding, as I said it, that I was delighted.

We sat down to the little dinner. Or rather I sat and she shuttled back and forth between the plain, solid kitchen table and the kind of Edwardian oven I remembered from my one visit to the Cloud House. I was not allowed to do anything except cut more of the scandalously fresh baguette. She produced each course without ceremony, deflecting attention away from the food with Paris chatter.

It served only to highlight how uniformly good it all was. Nessa hadn't forgotten how to cook. The main course was a Provençal stew. It looked a little too rustic to my eyes – my father's kind of food – but my eyes deceived me. How could a mere stew taste so sinfully good? I had thirds, and had to hold myself back from taking up her offer of fourths.

'Really, Nessa, it's such a shame that you've never opened a restaurant.'

She gave me a puckish smile. 'Never too late.'

I wiped my mouth. 'You mean you're considering it?'

A one-shoulder shrug. 'Georges and I are talking to some people.'

'Marvellous. I know it'll be a huge success. Beat the French at their own game.'

'Who said it would be in France?'

I leaned forward, putting her under amiable scrutiny.

'Nessa, don't tell me you mean Dublin.'

She shook her head, stiffening. 'No, not Dublin, Peter. Never Dublin.' She savoured the next word. 'Kinsale. Georges loves it there. Loves the sailing.'

'Really? Suzette never mentioned that you'd been down there with him.'

She sipped some still mineral water before answering. 'Suzette doesn't know everything.'

And there Nessa introduced her essential theme: what Suzette didn't know. She expanded upon it as we sat drinking double espressos in the lounging area after her perfectly judged crème brulée. Nessa smoked filterless cigarettes theatrically; she liked to flaunt her remaining vices. Another thing Suzette didn't know, her mother made it plain, was what was good for her. I was good for her, for example, and look what was happening in that department.

I sipped my pleasantly bitter coffee. 'But what can be done?' I asked, as if I were talking about a stranger's problem.

Nessa leaned forward on her black leather couch and stared at me earnestly with those glassy Kelly eyes she had given both of her children, the red eye of her cigarette staring at me too.

'Don't give up on her, Peter,' she said. 'Even if she rejects you again, don't give up. Deep down she craves this kind of attention. You've got to remember that Suzette is still recovering from her upbringing. She's still learning how to be a normal person. And you're the one to teach her, Peter Dagg. You're the one.'

I had a sceptical look frozen on my face. I wasn't at all sure I was the one. Not that I was going to further that discussion. Instead I said:

'Aren't you being a little hard on yourself, Nessa, saying Suzette didn't have a normal childhood? I mean, I know you had your troubles, especially later on. But I think you did a remarkably good job, considering . . . considering Jerry's track record.'

She sat back, her mouth wrinkling. When she stabbed out her unfinished cigarette, staring into the ashtray perched on the iron arm of the couch as if into a crystal ball, I knew I was in for a revelation. Oh Christ, I thought, why did I get involved with this family? Why did I have to break up with Una, my first love, the veterinarian's daughter?

Nessa said, 'No one knows better than I do that Jerry has got what he's always deserved these last few years.'

'I'm sure.'

'If it wasn't so difficult for my children, John Paul especially' – here she looked up at me sharply, as if I might doubt John Paul's capacity for pain – 'if it hadn't been for what they've gone through, what they're still going through, I might have enjoyed this spectacle.'

Her expression became rich. 'So you know I'm no friend of Jerry Mountain.'

'I know that, Nessa.'

She smiled nostalgically. 'I mean, the man told me he'd have me killed if I went through with the move to Paris.'

The lawyer in me stirred; the rest of me became quite still. 'He did, Nessa?'

She looked up at the exposed beams and laughed throatily. 'Said he knew some ex-IRA chaps here who might be interested in a little moonlighting.'

'This didn't . . . trouble you at all?' I knew Jeremiah Mountain, Jr. had already committed an offence by simply uttering those words, yet another for which he would never be convicted.

Nessa settled her face into a shrewd stare. 'Now, Peter, can you imagine a man less likely to know ex-members of the IRA than Jerry Mountain?'

I shook my head. Jerry had been called a West Brit so many times he wore it as a badge of pride. Then again, couldn't she see that a man like Jerry, who'd known power, might know anybody?

Laughing, I plagiarised my father's words, 'All the same, you have to admit he is an awful man.'

But Nessa's mood darkened. She took a bittersweet breath before speaking. 'I have to tell you, Peter, for the sake of honesty as much as for anything else, he wasn't the only one responsible for the whole bloody mess.'

I tried to cut the confession session short by saying, almost whispering: 'We all do things when we've been drinking, Nessa, that we're not proud of.' And I thought, Granny was right, I should have been a priest.

Nessa raised her eyebrows sharply, as if I'd given her a cue:

'Oh, I'm not talking about the drinking, Peter. I started sabotaging our marriage long before I started drinking in the morning.' She took a deep, deliberate breath. 'You see, I was first one to become unfaithful.' It was almost a boast.

I turned the rim of my roomy espresso cup, flicking Nessa a look that I hoped would tell her I didn't want to hear any more. If it did, it didn't stop her.

'In fact, for a while I wasn't completely sure who John Paul's father was. I thought it might have been' – and she mentioned the name of a well-known Irish journalist, someone who had been young and fresh in the sixties, as Nessa and Jerry had been, someone who had turned out to be a disappointment, as both of them had too.

'How did you eventually confirm Jerry's paternity?' I asked, thinking, Please tell me you did.

Nessa smiled, fondly. 'He grew into his father's looks. By the time he was four he was the spitting image.'

'Suzette you were always sure about?'

'Oh yes, Suzette was always her father's daughter. Lucky for her Jerry never found out, otherwise there might have been no Suzette at all.'

Imagine that, I thought: no Suzette. The prospect didn't frighten me in the absolute way it probably should have.

'Does she know about any of this?' I asked.

Nessa shook her head seriously. 'No. Not from me, anyway.'

'John Paul?'

'No.'

I put my cup and saucer down on the carved stand beside my armchair, decisively done. 'Then, with all due respect, Nessa, why are you telling me?'

'Because you need to know.'

'Why?'

'Because you're from the Owenstown Hill side of the family.' She laughed. 'We're the sensible ones.'

*　　*　　*

'If this barrister thing doesn't work out,' I told Nessa at the door, 'I hope you can give me a waitering job down in Kinsale.'

She shook her head. 'We'll be serving you at the grand opening. You and Suzette.'

I nodded, but didn't say anything. It was far easier to imagine Nessa and Georges opening their dream bistro than her daughter and I getting back together. A dark front – even lawyers have their Emily Dickinson moments – was advancing through my brain.

A few days after I left Paris Nessa was admitted to the American Hospital complaining of severe stomach pains. At first they thought she had an ulcer. Georges flew back from Frankfurt. Tests revealed cancer. Suzette flew in from Dublin. More tests revealed that the intestinal cancer was merely secondary; her liver was blotted with tumors. John Paul flew in from Prague, or, in another version of events I heard, Istanbul. She died the next day, back home in the apartment. Jerry flew in for the funeral.

Back out on the narrow rue des Saltimbanques I crossed over to the jeweller's window again. My eyes returned to one piece in particular, a silver bracelet on a velvet-draped stand. Its wide front with zigzagging lines of inlaid gold tapered to a delicate clasp at the back. It reminded me of a treasure I had seen in the National Museum in Dublin. It was very Suzette. The nine thousand franc price tag, indicated on a tiny block of plastic digits, did not put me off. In fact, it galvanised my resolve. I would make that investment, I would take that risk. Though it was now almost nine o'clock, the crystal door of the Galerie Malakov was still open.

As we drove up the feeder road (at freeway speed), I watched slogans form and dissolve on a screen just below the dealership's high sign:

Bob Wingate IS . . . Mr Discount
Summer Blow-out . . . Zero Money Down

John Paul swung into the dealership's surprisingly narrow entrance, putting on his indicator as an after-thought. We drove past the ranks of trucks and SUVs, past the Crystal Palace showroom, and parked in a reserved spot in front of Program Cars. Every customer parking space I could see was full; many of those guest cars and trucks looked as new as the gleaming vehicles on sale.

A salesman came down the steps of the showroom to greet us. He had a swollen face and a shell of prematurely greying hair. Tiny beads of sweat were struggling to migrate down his face. The salesman pulled a swollen hand out of his razor-creased, sheeny olive trousers and offered it with a punch to John Paul.

'Thought this was meant to be your day off, JP.'

John Paul counter-punched. 'Just stopping by, Marty, to show our friend here the ropes.' John Paul's voice had just got twangier, as if he were doing a mediocre impression of the salesman. Marty turned to me, grinning. 'You from Ireland too?'

'Yes, from Dublin.'

Marty's expression turned unexpectedly clever. 'We were beginning to think JP here was lying about where he hailed from.'

John Paul slapped his wet shoulder. 'We'll check you later, Marty.'

Inside was another planet – the light merry, the floor models cool to the touch, the air that of a spring morning. The vehicles seemed to glow from the depths of their own resinous bodies rather than glint and dazzle, as they did out in the raw sun. The biggest SUV, a dark blue elongated Tahoe, was in the middle of the marbly floor. Men in polo shirts and belted shorts walked around it, pausing to peer inside, as if it contained the bones of a saint. On a platform over by another glass wall two men sat behind computer terminals; a third, sharp-jawed and managerial, leaned over one of the screens. He looked up, saw John Paul and nodded with a tight smile. John Paul waved back, then said to me, 'The boys in the tower are a riot.'

I saw the boys in the tower exchanging words and smirks.

We weaved between customers and limited edition vehicles until we reached the far side of the showroom. Transparent offices sheltered beneath a mezzanine floor. From the largest office, right by the stairs, emerged a small man with a limp and a square beard. He wore a checked shirt and woollen tie, and looked like an Amish farmer with a suntan. He squinted up at us.

'Well, what do we have here?'

John Paul said, 'Steve, I'd like you to meet one of my oldest friends, and one of Ireland's finest young lawyers, Peter Dagg. Peter, meet Steve Dildine, General Manager, Wingate Chevrolet.'

I shook Dildine's small, leathery hand. He squinted back. 'A lawyer, hey?' The handshake was still going on, as if he could get a trace on me by prolonging the contact. He smiled, revealing a dental meltdown of a mouth. 'We sure don't have enough of those in Maverick.'

'A pleasure to meet you, Mr Dildine,' I replied, finally extracting my hand from his small trap.

Dildine turned to John Paul. Again that shrewd, toothless smile. 'Thinking of selling a unit or two to impress your friend here, Johnny?'

John Paul had taken off his shades, so I could see that he did not appreciate the question.

'No,' he replied coolly. 'Just bringing Peter up to the bridge. To see the Man.'

The general manager wasn't fazed. 'Well, don't let me stop you. I guess we'll see you back here Monday. For work, I mean.' Dildine took my hand again, this shake thankfully shorter, smoother. 'Nice to meet you, Irish. If you need some help in the transportation department, just give me a holler. Then again, John Paul here can always help you.' And he winked at my old friend.

'I'll keep that in mind, Mr Dildine.'

Was everybody a potential customer? Yes, of course they were.

As John Paul marched up the stairs ahead of me, I said, 'I appreciate you taking the day off for me.'

John Paul smiled over his shoulder. 'You're a good investment, Peter Dagg.'

The first office we came to, a dramatic space jutting out over the showroom, had a door that read, *Kristen Wingate-Mountain, Financing*. Wearing a sharp-shouldered grey jacket, she sat behind her desk, a young couple on the other side. Though they were all deep in paperwork, Kristen looked up and gave us a quality smile. 'We'll be through in about fifteen minutes, guys,' she said.

John Paul held up a reverent hand – a deal was being done here – and said, 'No problem. Plenty for Peter to see.'

We turned around. 'Let's go see Him instead,' John Paul whispered.

The office next door to Kristen's, closed and dark, said, *JP Mountain, Sales Coordinator*. I wondered what a Sales Coordinator did – after the reception he'd got on the floor, did he do anything? – but I wasn't about to ask. Besides, he was already leading me into the bridge's main office.

To my surprise, there was no secretary's sub-office, no buffer zone, between the door and Bob Wingate's desk. But inside Mr Discount, crowned with a headset, was holding court. A tall, intense short-sleeves-and-tie man, probably a manager, was standing behind Bob, making notes on some kind of invoice; two assistants were on our side of the desk, straining forward as if they were waiting to hear a punchline. Bob Wingate was very much the man from the billboard, with the addition of a three-dimensional presence like an overpowering aftershave, a little grey to the moustache, and curious half-moon bruises below his eyes, where bags might have formed on the face of another man in late middle age. He acknowledged his son-in-law with a smile and a quick hand gesture that looked like a pistol shot, but kept on talking:

'Bradley, I think we'll have to call an audible on that eighty-three moulding.'

That apparently was the punchline; one of the assistants walked around the desk and disappeared through a back passageway. John Paul turned to me. 'That's Brad Musslewhite he has on the line, used to be quarterback for the Brands in the Seventies.'

I tried to look impressed. Bob Wingate was already on another call. 'Rich, without the options package that's an incomplete. Think about it while I put you on hold, Coach.'

John Paul's quiet commentary: 'Rich Kickarillo – another dealer we're trying to do a ute exchange with.' I nodded.

Bob Wingate hit a flashing light on his console. 'Well, how the hell are you, Mr Radack! Me? Been getting away with it all day, sir, been getting away with it all day. Ready to come in and pick up that beauty?'

John Paul said, 'We've got twenty-four salesmen working here, Peter, not counting yours truly, and Bob still sells fifty to sixty units a month himself. A lot of the top clients, the Brad Musslewhites and the Jeff Radacks, they won't deal with anyone else.'

The Radack conversation went on for a long time, interrupted only by Bob putting him on hold to greet new callers with great exuberance, and great economy. With Radack, Bob went through a long list of reassurances, checking on his computer that a complex customisation had been completed. Nero would not have been pickier than Radack, but Bob handled the call with great aplomb and patience. Five minutes were devoted to the issue of leather trimming. I felt as if John Paul and I were waiting to see the headmaster at Berchmans. Kristen would be through with her customers before Bob would be ready to talk to us.

I had more than enough time to take in the big office. The shelves were crammed with sports trophies and memorabilia, golf and baseball predominating. The wood-panelled walls were largely obscured with sales plaques from corporate headquarters, family pictures, pictures of kids' sports teams with messages of gratitude for the dealership's sponsorship, and many beaming photos of Bob handing over the keys of very large vehicles to very large men. One oaky wall, however, was fairly bare. Was Bob Wingate leaving space for pictures of grandkids? If so, would John Paul and Kristen be furnishing him with those trophies any time soon? I remembered once overhearing John Paul say in the Europe Bar that he would rather have cancer than children. But then again, now that he'd taken up golf, surely any reversal of attitude was possible.

At last Bob's console was inactive. Taking off his headset, he turned to the remaining assistant and said, 'Dennis, tell Edmundo we're gonna have to punt on the special-edition Silverado.' Dennis didn't have to ask any questions; he nodded and left the bridge. The anxious manager said, 'I'll be in the war room, Bob.'

Now that he could give us his full attention, Bob made us the centre of his universe. He stood up and came around the wide glass-topped desk, revealing a gut that bulged like muscle. He didn't shake my hand: he engulfed it with both of his.

'Well, how are you, Coach?'

I wasn't at all sure what I coached but I replied positively, 'Just fine, Mr Wingate. It's good to be here.'

He looked at me with mock-gravity, or what I took to be mock-gravity, and said, 'Fielding error there, Pete, fielding error.'

'Pardon me?'

John Paul slapped me on the back. 'Means his father was Mr Wingate.'

'And most of the time he was plain Zeke,' Bob added.

Grateful for the translation, I said, 'It's good to be here, Bob.'

That seemed to cheer him no end. 'So what do you think of our single-platoon team, Coach?'

'The dealership? Oh, impressive, very impressive.'

'They got a franchise like this over in Ireland?'

'Not that I've seen.'

'John Paul give you the tour?'

'Yes indeed. It's all quite . . . vast.'

'Bet he didn't show you the dark side.'

I looked over at John Paul. There was no humour in his smile. 'No, no,' I replied. 'I don't believe he has.'

Bob jabbed his son-in-law's ribs with a thick forefinger. 'I like to josh him about this, Pete. You see, John Paul here isn't too crazy about the nitty-gritty part of the operation. Not that I can blame him. Guess you have to grow up with it to really love the oil and grease. Personally, if I had a choice, I'd be mechanicing from sunup to sundown.'

John Paul added, 'In other words, my father-in-law is itching to show you the shop.'

I noticed two red lights pulsing on the console.

'I really wouldn't want to take Bob away from his work,' I replied.

'Nonsense, Coach, I can get someone off the bench to take care of things while we take a little tour.'

So that is how I found myself trailing Suburban Bob through the bowels of the bridge. John Paul had excused himself from the tour, claiming that he did have a few things to take care of in his office. I was glad of that, sensing that I could take quiet advantage of this time alone with my quarry's boss.

We went through what I took to be the war room the manager had referred to earlier. On the walls were Salesman of the Month plaques dating back to the seventies, and a whiteboard with a dense grid recording unit sales for the current month. Each of the plentiful check marks looked like the Nike trademark swoop. But there were no swoops, nor anything else, beside John Paul's name.

Bob held open a brown metal door for me and we walked down a steep, clanging flight of stairs into a long warehouse that Bob called the stock room. Rows of pallet racks rose almost to the top of the distant aluminium ceiling. A forklift burdened with what looked like an entire engine sped towards us along the nearest alley.

'This way, Coach,' said Bob, veering left.

We went through another door into a waiting area with blue plastic seats, where a woman with an eighties perm standing behind a counter shouted, 'Well, and how are you today then, Bob?'

'Gooder than heck, Sandy,' he replied serenely, 'gooder than heck.' He turned to me. 'Service centre next stop.'

We went through a glass door, and entered a different business. It was noisy, it was hot, it was labour. Most of the roll-up doors on the left-hand side were raised, letting in all the humidity but not much of the light. Bob pointed and lectured:

'Each mechanic has his own bay, his own chest of tools. When I retire I think I'm going to park myself at that one there Rogelio's working at, kick him upstairs.'

Rogelio, a young Hispanic in the standard-issue brown overalls, looked up from the engine he was working on and nodded confidently at us. Other mechanics we passed – I caught names like Lance, WP, Hermes on their white patches – seemed too busy to even notice us. The vehicles they were working on looked as new as any in the lot.

I said, 'I trust that's not going to be for a long time.'

'What's that, Coach?'

'Until you retire.'

'Well, it won't be for ever. Now that we have a relief pitcher warming up I can see I won't have to be there for the ninth.'

I said, 'In other words . . .'

Bob put a heavy hand on the back of my neck. I readied myself for a revelation.

'In other words,' he said, 'some day I'll be hitting that sacrifice fly.'

Was this an allusion, I wondered, to the Truck Nation offer? Bob slapped my shoulder blade. 'This way, Coach. Time to check out the collision centre.'

We turned right and pushed through a pair of metallic swing doors. The collision centre was another long workshop, but brighter and cleaner than the service centre. A pervasive groaning sound began to grate on my nerves.

'What's that noise, Bob?'

'Compressor. On the go twenty-four seven. Because of the dreaded bond dust.'

'The what dust?'

'Bond. Secret of our success.'

Bob went over to an SUV raised chest-high on hydraulics and pointed out the white paste bordering a sandy rectangle on the front passenger door.

That damage was cosmetic compared to the other four vehicles we passed, all of them in various stages of de- and reconstruction, except the last: a smallish blue car, the back end of which had been shredded.

'Surely that one is a genuine write-off,' I said.

Bob shook his head with a smile. 'You'd be surprised the magic we can work with wrecks.'

Ah, I wanted to tell him, but I've already seen evidence of that in New Plantation.

Bob stopped by a small office marked *Dispatcher* and had a quick, loud conversation with a diminutive woman in a loose shirt called Beth Ann. A pyramid of paint cans was stacked against the back wall. Beth Ann accompanied us as we did the last leg of the tour, a long space called the paint room. 'This is where we finish up strong,' Bob said. 'Finish up strong.'

We went through the preparation area, which smelled like a hot, greasy kitchen; then the paint dispensing area, where polished metal taps looked as if they would deliver heavy squirts of ketchup and mustard. Bob spent more time talking shop with Beth Ann and less time providing commentary to me: he was getting back to work. If I was to exploit my time with him, I would have to do it soon.

We stopped in front of a thickly glazed chamber built in the middle of the shop floor. The front doors, fringed with fat black rubber, were mounted on tracks and stood open. Standing inside was a broad green car, smothered in cloudily transparent sheeting and white masking tape, except for a sandy, bond-bordered square above the left front wheel. A technician wearing a mask was crouched down beside the repair, spraying it deep green again with a high-powered gun.

'She'll be ready for baking after lunch.'

'Baking?'

'Yes, Coach, this is the kiln. Let me show you.'

We left Beth Ann watching over the spray-painter and entered a rudimentary control booth on the right. Bob stood at a waist-high panel of primitive knobs, gauges, and switches.

'Flick a few of these,' he says, 'and it gets up to a hun'red and sixty-five degrees in there.'

Beginning to feel that heat, I put a hand on the cool metal panel. 'I had no idea,' I said.

He turned to me. 'And you know what you have after three hours?'

'What, Bob?'

His billboard smile. 'Perfect execution.'

I trusted he was still using sports metaphors.

'You know, Bob, I still can't quite get over it.'

He had been staring at the wrapped car, but now his eyes snapped back to me, those half-moons beneath them looking darker than before.

'Can't quite get over what, Coach?'

I showed him an undesigning face. 'John Paul – my friend – selling cars for a living. Not, you know, the trade in which he was brought up.'

Bob frowned. 'Far as I can make out, Pete, he wasn't brought up in any kind of trade at all. Lucky for him that he married into a family that's a business, and a business that's a family.'

'Yes, lucky indeed.' There was a silence, which I broke by saying, 'Do you suppose he'll stick with it?'

Bob's face lightened. 'Stick with it! Coach, that boy's the next president of Wingate Chevrolet. In this family he's just like your Prince Charles.'

I wanted to explain to him that he was not my Prince Charles, but this control booth, and that chamber, were making me sweat. I am not claustrophobic, but I was beginning to feel claustrophobic there.

'Well,' I said, 'I suppose we shouldn't make the prince wait any longer. Thanks for the tour, Mr Wingate.'

Bob looked at me with a shrewd eye. 'No, Coach, thank you for coming.'

Later, as John Paul, Kristen, and I were going down the front steps, finally on our way out to lunch, John Paul said, 'So, Peter, now that you've been up close and personal with my father-in-law, did you notice anything weird?'

'Oh, John Paul,' Kristen fondly rebuked him.

I didn't know what to say, or what to say first.

'No, nothing weird exactly.'

'Not even those bruises?'

'Under his eyes? Well, yes, in fact, I did notice those.'

John Paul turned to his wife. 'See how good he is with details, my dear. No wonder they sent him.'

I put the conversation back on track:

'Well, the bruises would have been hard to miss – sorry, Kristen.'

'No apology necessary,' she replied. 'If Dad wants to do that to himself, it's fine by me.'

'To himself?' I said.

'Yep,' answered John Paul, taking out his Blazer remote. 'Mr Discount has had a lot more plastic surgery than Mrs Discount.'

That afternoon John Paul took me to the Culture District. When he'd suggested we go there, over lunch at Instant Gourmet!, I said something like: 'Is that the only place in this town where that carry-on is legal?', which he didn't appreciate, though I did catch Kristen smiling to herself as she stabbed her crammed salad.

I developed this little theory that Maverick was like a religion. Kristen, brought up in the faith, was at ease with it, and had the confidence to take from it what she wanted. Her husband had only the dogma of the convert.

But he was rightfully proud of the Culture District, I'll give him that. The Culture District was something else. Maverick had commissioned each of the world's greatest architects, the Olympian postmodernists, the big names that even I was familiar with, to build a gallery or extension. Besides the big museums, there were quirkier collections dedicated to movements I had never heard of, such as Mexican Futurism and Garbage Art; tiny non-denominational chapels called sacred spaces adorned with moody non-representational art; 'not-for-profit' organisations housed in wood-and-brick cottages; small restaurants, quaint cafés – all washed by a neat sea of grass: in the Culture District you had to park your ute and walk.

I was suitably impressed by the Maverick Museum of Modern Art's Fauve holdings and the Maverick Museum of Fine Art's almost authenticated Titian, but the exhibits I really warmed to were in a place that I barely thought worth a visit – the Art Car Museum; John Paul's enthusiasm won me over. Once there I had a hard time deciding which was my favourite: the pyramid car, or the butterfly car, or the Elvis low-rider, though in the end the Mount Rushmore truck, in a room of its own, took the biscuit.

I bought postcards of them all, intending to write deadpan

messages home about Maverick and Maverickians; I couldn't let Dublin know that I was beginning to like the place, now could I?

We were both tired from our culture hike – the frigid air inside, the humidity outside – and so we ordered cappuccinos in the museum café and sat across from each other in a booth fashioned from the innards of a Cadillac. I have to admit that it wasn't exactly the kind of ambiance I'd imagined for one of my softly, softly interrogations, but I suppose strangers can't be choosers.

I said, 'Tell me about Kristen.'

He tried his frothy coffee before answering. 'What do you want to know?'

'Well, when did you know you wanted to marry her? For that matter, when did you know you wanted to marry?'

He was very pleased with the second question.

'What's this! Don't tell me you're getting cold feet, Peter.'

This reversal startled me. I shook my head.

'Me? No. Of course not.' I laughed. 'This is all about you, John Paul.'

'I'm flattered. Let me put it this way.' He stirred his drink slowly with a fat spoon. 'You can't know how lost you are until you meet someone who has a compass.'

'Oh, come on now. Things weren't that directionless in the Mountain household . . . surely.'

John Paul leaned towards me, staring.

'I slept with Nessa.'

I said nothing, just adjusted the angle of my head several times, hoping that would help me say something.

John Paul leaned back laughing. 'Look at you,' he said. 'I think you enjoy thinking the worst about us. No, when I say I slept with her I literally mean I *slept* with her, in their bed.'

I wished he would keep his voice down. Almost in a whisper I asked, 'Where was Jerry?'

He threw a hand up. 'That's the point. Jerry was out screwing for Ireland – or so I later figured out – and my poor mother was so lonely that she had to ask a ten-year-old boy to come fill his space. Some mornings I would wake up and go to my bedroom and find him crashed out on my bed, still in his suit, still in his shoes.'

After a silence, I asked, 'Does Suzette know about this?'

'Of course Suzette knows.'

'I see,' I said.

And I did see. I was beginning to see.

'Impressive,' I said.

John Paul laughed. I looked at him over my shoulder.

'Not impressive?'

He snorted. 'You should see where the rich people live.'

'This isn't rich?'

'Magnolia Bend makes this place look like a ghetto.'

'Where's Magnolia Bend?'

'Inside the Beltway,' he replied, slouched elegantly in the back seat of the Blazer. 'Where the old Maverick money lives.'

'Some of it made as far back as the seventies,' added Kristen.

'Hey now,' protested John Paul, the pious Maverickian.

Ignoring him, Kristen told me, 'My mother thinks she's missing out on some opportunities by staying here.'

'Such as?'

'Well,' Kristen answered with relish, 'last year she chaired her first disease dinner, the Allergy Research Gala Ball. It went well but this year she's only been offered Lower Back Pain.'

'Can't get the big diseases.'

'Exactly.'

'Magnolia Bend is a pathological paradise,' John Paul explained. 'They get all the big killers. Cancer, heart disease, strokes – take your pick.'

'Maybe not cancer, love,' Kristen protested. 'You'd have to live on the Boulevard to be in line for that.'

The relative ghetto we were driving through was Logan Hollow, the suburb where Kristen and her siblings had grown up and her parents still lived. According to the mild wooden sign we'd passed a few streets back, it was, in full, the City of Logan Hollow, Incorporated 1959. That move had been necessary, Kristen explained, to avoid being swallowed up by the sprawling monster that was Maverick, a tax monster with a ravenous appetite. Back then all this – the long blocks of huge colonial houses, the tent of high pines, the polished light – had been nothing more than farmland and a few pioneering subdivisions of ranch houses. Even when the Wingates had moved here in the late seventies there was a field behind their house where a neighbour kept a pet buffalo.

But there was no longer any room for buffalo to roam in Logan Hollow, though it still didn't look much like a city to me. Where were the eyesores, where were the monuments, where were my clients? I had a flash of nostalgia: Dublin – now *that* was a city, for better or for worse.

We drove at a stately pace through the affluent hush, and not just because Kristen was a more cautious driver than her husband; if you went a notch over thirty here, according to John Paul himself, more than likely you would be stopped and given a one-hundred-dollar ticket – pocket money, presumably, in this neck of the woods – by the ubiquitous City of Logan Hollow Police; already two of their dent-free white cruisers had prowled by us.

I was thankful for their chaperoning. Our reasonable speed allowed me a leisurely gawk at the houses rolling by: dormer windows; white Doric pillars; wings reminiscent of carriage houses, with an SUV, the new carriage, stationed beneath each high arch.

The larger the house, the fewer signs of life in the windows. On the evening streets the only people to be seen were a few middle-aged women in Spandex gripping small grey weights and waddle-walking furiously with tunnel-vision focus; and, on every second block, Mexican labourers – stocky men with cured faces –

loading up lawnmowers onto battered pick-up trucks bristling with spades and trimmers.

We turned left into the Wingates' street, a shady enclave called Pecan Circle. Here the red-brick mansions were a little more modest, and the house we pulled up at was not a pseudo-Georgian pile at all. I had noted a few other architectural aberrations since we'd nosed into Logan Hollow – the odd failed example of glassy modernism, a couple of hacienda-style houses, even a few long wood-and-brick bungalows, the original ranch houses that Kristen had mentioned.

The Wingates' place was a ranch house too, or at least it had begun that way. As Kristen told me when we got out of the Blazer, 'My parents went a bit crazy on extensions. They built the second storey and that wing of bedrooms in eighty-one, the sun room in my senior year of high school.' She was pointing to a large pentagon of windows and chandelier light that fronted the other flank of the expansive house: their domestic showroom. I saw Bob Wingate himself – he didn't need a billboard to be recognisable at a distance – walking across the room towards the front door.

'And they've extended deep too,' John Paul murmured profoundly. 'They've extended deep.'

The busily bevelled front door swung open as we set foot on the low porch and Bob's bulging hand crossed the threshold.

'See you found us, Coach.'

'Indeed, Bob,' I replied.

We stepped inside the milky marble hallway. An angular, petite woman came through a doorway from the cavernous back of the house. She had big credulous brown eyes, and a canopy of brown hair with spiky blonde highlights: borderline big hair. She must have been hitting fifty, but her pale, lightly made-up face was suspiciously free of wrinkles. The effect could have been from a before-and-after advert for a miracle rejuvenating product. Helen Wingate was the after picture.

'Hi, guys,' she said, giving me a cute stare.

I shook her slim hand. 'Nice to meet you, Mrs Wingate.'

She grasped mine. 'Oh, don't you dare call me Mrs Wingate, Peter Dagg. You Irish are so formal! John Paul was the same way for the first few weeks, bless him. No – it's Helen, or out you go!'

I wasn't thrown out. Instead I was the guest of honour.

At dinner the carved mahogany dining table gleamed as brilliantly as any model on Suburban Bob's showroom floor.

We got on to talking about the various dignitaries that Wingate Chevy, as corporate sponsor and under the auspices of the president's wife, had helped bring to Maverick.

I said, 'So tell me about Nelson Mandela, Helen.'

'He was charming. Such charisma. You felt you were in the presence of a truly great man.'

Her husband was mopping up the dregs of the ineffably good marinara sauce that had covered our entrée (as Americans insist on calling their main course).

'My all-time favourite is the Dalai Lama,' he offered. 'Man, that guy was a stitch.'

Kristen looked mildly embarrassed. John Paul was busy with his Merlot. I took it upon myself to change the subject:

'John Paul brought me to the Culture District today, Helen,' I said. 'I was impressed. I had no idea there was so much going on in Maverick.'

Helen's eyes had become earnestly circular. 'And what you saw was just the tip of the iceberg, Peter. Just the very tip. Did you know that University of Maverick has the top-rated creative non-fiction programme in the country?'

'I didn't.'

'Or that when he's not in Maverick, Maestro Faustbender is in Vienna conducting the Austrian National Broadcasting Orchestra?'

'I had no idea.'

'We could have the bloody Renaissance going on down here,'

84

John Paul grumbled, 'and people in New York would still think culture in Maverick resembles the banjo scene in *Deliverance*.'

I laughed, Mr and Mrs Wingate nodded, but Kristen's stillness betrayed a certain irritation. Perhaps she'd heard John Paul make that quip before. Perhaps it was a displaced kind of irritation. It was easy to imagine a whole reservoir of resentment building against John Paul Mountain. It had happened in Dublin.

'How long are you going to be in Maverick, Peter?' Helen asked.

'Till Tuesday.'

'Going back to Ireland so soon?'

'Well, no, I'm going to be in the States for the rest of the month, in fact. Irish friends in San Francisco have invited me to stay.'

'Can't you change your reservation and stay with us a little bit longer? There's a wonderful Matisse exhibition opening at MMAM next week.'

'Actually, I'm not flying.'

'Not flying?'

'No, I was thinking of renting a car and driving to the West Coast. Something I've always wanted to do. *On The Road* and all that.'

'Well, you can forget about renting a car,' Bob said matter-of-factly, as he dished himself a few more veal cutlets. 'You can take one from us.'

'That's very kind of you, Bob. But I don't think I'll be able to make it back to Maverick.'

Suburban Bob dismissed this quibble with curt wave of his thick hand. 'We don't need it back.'

'But what would I do with the car in California?'

'Sell it – it's yours.'

John Paul said, 'Don't you see, Peter? Suburban Bob wants to give you a car.'

Bob nodded absent-mindedly as he sliced up his meat.

'But really, I couldn't, Mr Wingate. That's too generous.'

Bob made a mild halt sign. 'Come by Monday. I'll tell Steve Dildine to set you up.'

'And since you'll have your own wheels, Peter,' John Paul said, 'why don't you stick around a little bit longer than Tuesday. We'd love to have you.'

'Yes,' Kristen said. 'We'd love to have you.'

But talk of love made me think more like a lawyer. Why would they love to have me?

'I'm sure your friends in San Francisco wouldn't mind if you were a few days late,' Helen added. 'And I'd love to take you to that Matisse exhibition. There really is a lot more for you to do in Maverick.'

'And a lot more to talk about,' John Paul said, looking at me archly as he lifted his wine glass.

I looked at all of them, these formidable and determined hosts ranged around the table, and replied, 'How could I say no? I'd love to stay longer.'

And the odd thing was that as I said it I realised I really did want to stay. I needed more than another three days to get to know John Paul Mountain, and his new world, properly. I had unfinished business and unfinished pleasure in Maverick, Texas.

Later, much later, John Paul and I were sitting out by the Wingates' pool – tastefully tiled, tastefully lit, and not ostentatious in size – drinking margaritas expertly concocted by Bob. The mosquitoes had driven the others inside, and although I was suffering, I didn't want to lose this opportunity to talk while John Paul was in a talking mood. There were questions I wanted answers to, though not for the right reasons; at least, not for the reasons I had come out here with. I was not asking them for Suzette's sake.

I said, 'I still don't understand something, John Paul.'

'What don't you understand, Peter?'

'I can understand – provisionally – why you might not want to make peace with Jerry and Suzette, but what about Dublin? Is Dublin really that bad?'

He grunted a laugh, and stared out into the night before replying, 'Did I ever tell you about going to the Subterraneans?'

The Subterraneans, I knew, were an improv. comedy troupe who performed in a cellar bar on Dame Street. I knew because they'd recently hired Suzette to do some PR work. They were the comedians she was going off to see the day she'd asked me to be her Maverick ambassador.

'No, I don't believe you have,' I replied.

'One night – right in the middle of all the tragic shit that was going down – myself and Iremonger went to see them. Early in the show the MC asks the audience for the name of a soap opera and some prick at the back yells out the Mountains, to tremendous applause.' He turned and stared at me. 'Seeing your pain acted out on a crappy little stage in the style of film noir, *Star Trek* and Mentos ads – that's Dublin.'

I looked down at the plastic table between us. 'Did you have to stay?' I asked quietly.

'No, no I didn't – and that's why I'm here.'

'I meant—'

'I know what you meant, Peter. In fact, Tom got me out of that hole before I could do some serious damage to someone, or to myself. You see, it's not the shitheads of Dublin I'm scared of – it's myself. I'm scared of my Dublin self.'

After a few moments, I asked, 'But is there really any such person?'

He looked at me sideways. 'Oh yes, Peter, and if I'd stayed with him I think I would have killed someone by now, or killed myself.'

'You seriously thought of doing that?'

He disturbed me further by laughing. 'Before Kristen, oh sure. I remember in particular this summer night in Berlin when I ended up alone on this high balcony. Have you ever had one of those moments, Peter, when you're so drunk that you see your life with utter clarity?'

I shook my head apologetically. 'No, John Paul, I can't say I have.'

He sighed. 'No, I suppose you haven't. But anyway, there I was, on the sixth-floor of this grim apartment building, seriously tempted by the idea of the big jump, when I thought, Just because I want to end my life doesn't mean I have to die.'

'I don't quite follow,' I said.

He leaned towards me.

'Why not change lives? That's what I thought.'

'What,' I replied, 'you mean just like changing suits?'

'Exactly!'

I shook my head. 'But John Paul . . .'

'But John Paul what?'

My turn to sigh. 'Nothing – it is your life.'

'Yes it is,' he replied, as if we saw eye to eye. He stood up and looked around – at the dark, humming gardens, the illuminated rockeries with their satyrs and centaurs, the pool, the high windows of the house. Calmly he added, 'And you can see why I like it here.'

'Yes, John Paul. Anyone would like it here.'

'Would you do me a favour?'

'Of course.' Was this going to be a message for his sister, his father even?

'I have this irresistible urge for a swim. Would you go back inside and ask Helen for a large towel?'

I stood up. 'All right.' Did every Mountain regard me as a messenger?

When he stood up I thought he was going to dive in fully clothed, but at the edge he started to strip down to his boxer shorts. They were black. I turned around on the deck and watched him execute a crisp dive from the board. A lone neighbourhood dog took note of it.

I watched him surface and then went inside.

Kristen, John Paul, and I were in these droning World War II fighters, flying wingtip to wingtip through a Texan blue sky . . . on our way to strafe the Four Courts. We didn't reach our target. I woke up to discover the droning, at least, was real. The time – 4:37 – glowed red in the dark from the bedside table. I sat up and listened more attentively. The droning was no car or truck engine. And I couldn't even tell which side of the house it was coming from. It grew loud, then faded, grew loud, then faded, over and over again. If I had been at home in my own bed, I don't think I would have been bothered to find out what it was. But I wasn't at home. I got out of my foreign bed, went to the window, and swivelled the slats of the blind open. No sign of anything in the dark back garden, or out on the black fairway.

Slipping on a pair of jeans and a T-shirt, I left the guest room, crossed the bridge, and made my way down the stairs quietly – easy in a house without creaks. My bare feet made sticky steps over the cool marble at the bottom of the stairs. I peeked out through the slats of a front window. Suspended in a kind of aquarium light, Pocahontas Lane was absolutely still. But I could still hear that droning.

This was one mystery, I decided, that would have to wait for daylight. I crept back up the stairs. Back on the landing I noticed a knife of light at the end of the corridor: John Paul's study. Perhaps his sleep had been disturbed by the droning too. I went over to the door and was just about to tap on it – no point in startling him – when it swung open, the full light stinging my eyes, and the muzzle of a gun pointing in my face.

'Shite, no!' I roared.

John Paul, fully dressed, lowered the gun and roared with laughter.

'Fear brings out the Dubliner in you, Peter.'

'Would you mind putting that thing away,' was all I could manage to say.

Kristen came running up the stairs, wrapping a silk dressing gown around a thigh-length T-shirt. She was very sleepy and very disturbed.

'John Paul, what the hell is going on?'

'I'm just putting the Sauer away, dear,' he replied, as though he were talking about the vacuum cleaner. 'I thought our guest was an intruder.'

He turned around and walked over to the desk where he had been working on the computer. (*Was* he writing that memoir?)

Kristen was shaking her head. 'I'm sorry, Peter. I really am so sorry.'

'Don't apologise, please. No harm done. What is it that your father said over dinner: no blood, no foul.' Despite my attitude, my laughter was nervy.

John Paul was back, empty-handed. 'I should apologise, Peter, I know. I am sorry. Didn't mean to scare ya. But frankly I didn't think you'd be prowling around the house at five in the morning.'

Kristen had slipped back downstairs without another word. I surprised myself by thinking, it was worth being terrified just to see her so intimately.

I said to her husband, 'I heard this droning noise that wouldn't stop.'

Of course, now it had stopped. John Paul laughed again.

'You mean the mosquito truck. The sprayers do make quite a noise, if you're not used to it.'

'They spray at this time of night?'

'No better time. I told you they were good around here.'

'Apparently.' I tried to look past him. 'So what are you doing up at this hour?' His computer screen was glowing, but I could not make out the text.

He shrugged. 'Early riser.'

'That's all?'

'That's all.'

'Well, I for one am going back to sleep, if I can.'

John Paul seemed happy to hear it.

'Coffee will be ready when you wake up, friend.'

When I did wake up again, I knew it was time to give Suzette another update. I didn't need to fish out the GreenGlobe card again – the Law has given me an over-retentive memory.

'It's me.'

'Peter.' The warmth and relief in her voice – for a moment this conversation was all about us. And I wasn't sure what contribution I had to make.

But I knew that talk would quickly turn to business, family business. When she said, 'How are you doing?' I understood that she wasn't inquiring about my health.

'I think I'm making progress,' I replied.

'What kind of progress, sweetie?'

I thought, I'm beginning to see things from his point of view.

I said, 'He's beginning to see things from our point of view.'

'Oh . . . excellent.' She seemed surprised. But if she was, why had she sent me in the first place? She added, 'Have you mentioned the wedding?'

'Mentioned it, yes.'

'And?'

I sighed. 'Don't expect miracles.'

'Oh, I don't, sweetie. I'm sorry. I'm sure you're doing a great job. But what maybe can we expect by Tuesday?'

'Suzette, I'm staying longer.'

'How much longer?'

'As long as it takes.'

'But what about Garrett and Katy in San Francisco?'

'I phoned them last night. They were great about it. Said they'd still be there.'

'Well, absolutely,' Suzette said lightly. The tone she was taking was for her one of high diplomacy. 'Whatever you think is right. But, tell me, who suggested it, staying longer?'

I laughed dryly. 'I dropped a lot of hints, and finally got the extended invitation. But I'll be on the road by the end of the week. I'm sure of it.'

That was my last perjurious statement of the conversation, except perhaps when I told Suzette how much I missed her.

Sunday driving.

We were only on the freeway a couple of miles before John Paul exited and turned onto a broad street called Sergeant Garcia-Rameau Drive.

According to John Paul, SilverScreen 36 was the largest multiplex in the world. It didn't look too different to the one back home in Tallaght, just a few extra wings and a very busy façade heavy on purple girders and orange perspex. The building was crowned, for some reason, with half a dozen ocean liner funnels. The plaza in front was a melting pot of baggily dressed teenagers. I spotted Kristen sitting by a fountain. She had a kiss for both of us.

'Tickets?' asked John Paul.

'Have them already,' Kristen replied brightly.

I couldn't express any enthusiasm. An hour earlier I had played a politely minor role in the decision-making process on what movie to see – conducted on the move, mobile to mobile. True, I had vetoed the 'screwball comedy' on the shortlist, but hadn't said a word against the thriller Kristen liked the sound of and John Paul was clearly set on. In Dublin he had never gone to see movies, he'd gone to see films.

What had happened to that art-house animal, the subtitle maso-chist who liked to prove his bohemian credentials by sitting through Tarkofsky double-bills, Renoir retrospectives? Who or what had killed him?

Looked as if he had done it himself: it was suicide.

Inside the megaplex – sensory assault: the cacophony of an amusement arcade on one side of the ticket checkpoint, and a bank of video screens on the other playing booming trailers. A boy wearing a plastic bowtie gave us directions to Screen 34. We went right, then left, then right again, past a fast-food niche with polished steel fixtures, two Tensa-barrier stub checks, and three concession stands before we finally reached the door with the stylised title of our selection. We had turned into a caravan of junk food along the way.

When the opening credits for the feature film began to roll – how many different companies does it take to make a movie? – John Paul put his giant soda back in its holder and, without saying a word, got up and left the theatre. I presumed he was just going to use the bathroom, but when he didn't return after ten minutes (six or seven major characters had already been murdered in graphic and grisly ways), I turned to Kristen and said: 'Did your husband flee the building?'

Unconcerned, she finished munching some popcorn before reply-ing: 'Oh, he often does this.'

She did not take her eyes, green again in the movie light, off the screen.

'Often does what?'

'Goes looking for other previews.'

'Why?'

'He prefers the preview to the full movie. Plus he gets a kick out of sneaking into all the other theatres without getting caught.'

'Well, that's a bit antisocial, isn't it?'

She shrugged, munching more popcorn. 'John Paul likes to get his money's worth.'

'No, I mean, leaving you alone.'

Now she took her eyes off the action.

'I have you here chaperoning me, don't I?'

I turned back to the turgid entertainment, smiling at it for once. Yes, she had me.

It would be another hour until John Paul reappeared – just in time for the movie's transcendentally violent climax. For that time I fairly hummed with Kristen's presence. I was even blissfully immune to the movie's contagious crappiness. Besides, she was enjoying it. It was to be the happiest hour I spent in Maverick.

That Sunday night, in the privacy of their living room, we watched a much better film.

Because they had met in Paris the dress was from Galeries Lafayette, bought on a shopping expedition Kristen and her mother mounted a month after John Paul had proposed on the Japanese footbridge at Giverney. I'm no fashion expert, but even I could tell, leaving aside what Kristen and her figure brought to it, that the dress was stunning – simple, trim and elegant, with just the right degree of sparkle. Beneath the lightest of veils Kristen's bone-blonde hair was done up chignon-style, her wide American features distilled with discreet make-up. What could I say? I had to say something. The truth:

'Beautiful.'

Kristen, sitting forward on the slim leather couch beside me, hands clasping one folded leg, tilted her head and said, 'Thank you, Peter.'

I glanced over at John Paul, slouched deep in an armchair, bottle of Shiner Bock in hand. He looked quite absorbed in the video, a mild smile on his lips.

This was no home movie. The wedding had been a big production; the video record of it was a big production. It had titles, effects, its own soundtrack. The editing was slick. The company

Bob hired, John Paul had informed me, spent most of its time making fund-raising videos for private universities. After watching this polished documentary – *Kristen and John Paul's Day* – I was ready to donate.

It was very much, as my father says about pictures he didn't like, a director's film. Flowers were the chief motif. There was a series of jump cuts between the bride and floating islands of tropical blossoms in the illuminated pool at the Wingates' house, where the Hawaiian-themed rehearsal dinner had been the night before. In the garden of the Logan Hollow Country Club, a tracking shot brought us down the red carpet, canopied with roses; it led to the gazebo where the non-denominational ceremony took place. A hand-held camera wandered around the empty ballroom inside, dwelling on the garlanded pillars, sweeping the petal-strewn floor. I shuddered to think how much the flowers alone had cost.

There were fauna as well as flora. Kristen did have equal billing with the flowers, though I would have liked to have seen a lot more of her. The groom, in his matching golden-brown cravat and waistcoat, looked every inch the smooth leading man, playing his part with great charm, careful not to upstage his lady. Helen, wearing a trim cream suit and a hat with just the right degree of attitude, cried on cue, but not outrageously. Bob filled the screen every time he came on, the way he filled his conservative tuxedo. Proud as punch, he looked as if he had just sold a limited edition truck.

The boys from Dublin were given some screen time too, though I suspect most of their scenes were left on the cutting room floor. Against the backdrop of would-be society ladies and bland professionals, young and old, John Paul's cronies emerged as the comic relief. They could be trusted to pull a face or perform some alcoholic stunt any time the camera turned on them. There was the inevitable shot of Iremonger being thrown in the pool, obliterating one of the floral islands.

I said, 'I hope all these Texans didn't get the wrong idea about Irish people.'

'Don't worry, they did,' Kristen answered.

'Pity there couldn't have been a more . . . representative sample there.'

'Pity my father is afraid to fly,' John Paul answered, and slugged his Shiner Bock.

Well, that was his story. I knew how the invitation game had really played out.

Jerry was living in a flat in Harold's Cross, where he had moved after losing the Cloud House; Suzette and the former treasurer of the Dinner Party were helping him with the rent, though how much help he really needed only an omniscient accountant could have told us.

Word got back to Dublin, as it always does, about John Paul's engagement. Suzette tracked her brother down by phone in New York and offered him tense congratulations. Things had not been healthy between them – they hadn't seen each other – since their mother's funeral. John Paul accepted her congratulations laconically, and was vague about wedding plans. Somewhere, sometime in Texas, he said, before killing the call.

Then the Iremongers of Dublin started to get not only their invitations – tall off-white cards, handwritten in swirling calligraphy, waved ironically yet proudly around pubs – but also return plane tickets to Maverick. This was no simple plea for presents. The people John Paul wanted to come he wanted to come.

No fancy envelopes from Texas came through the letterbox at Jerry's apartment or his daughter's. They responded with curt sarcasm. Jerry took to referring to his son, when he referred to him at all, as JR. Suzette was less charitable still, calling him the Tumbleweed.

One summer morning I did a double-take on Dawson Street when I spotted John Paul coming out of Hodges Figgis. This time there was none of his random-meeting nonchalance. He crossed to the Waterstone's side so urgently that he was almost mowed down by the charging one-way traffic.

Later we learned he was back in Dublin getting his emigration papers in order for the American embassy, and keeping as low a profile as he could before his interview date.

'I hope no one misses the irony of that son of mine being able to produce a Certificate of Good Character from the Gardaí,' Jerry commented over supper at Suzette's one night. I wasn't sure which of the multiple ironies in that sentence he was highlighting.

'Well, he's never been arrested by the *Irish* police,' Suzette said.

'I should have phoned my old friend Mundow of the Drugs Squad while I had the chance,' Jerry replied.

Then, just when we had all given up unspoken hope, two invitations appeared in Jerry's postbox. Forwarded from the Cloud House, they were addressed, in that infallible artistic hand, to Mr Jeremiah John Mountain and Guest and Miss Suzette Catherine Mountain and Guest.

The heavy, linen-textured cards began:

Mr and Mrs Robert Travis Wingate, junior
request the honour of your presence
at the marriage of their daughter

Kristen Ashlyn
to
Mr John Paul Michael Mountain

The wedding date was thirteen days away.

'Where are the bloody plane tickets?' Jerry seethed, as if he were a frequent flyer.

'Perhaps they're on their way,' I suggested.

Jerry shook his head. 'No they're not. This is John Paul's idea of a big statement. They've probably pressured him into inviting us – I'm sure they're decent people, for Americans – but he's ensured that we don't have a practical means of getting there. He's flying Tom Iremonger over, but not his own flesh and blood.'

'Wouldn't you have some difficulty with flying to Texas, even if he had put in a ticket, Jerry?' I ventured cautiously.

He threw up his hands melodramatically. 'Oh, Jesus, I have no intention of going, even if he Fed-Exes me a ticket for Concorde. And even if I adored being thirty-nine feet off the good earth I'm not sure I'd want to go. That fella has a lot to answer for. The way he behaved after his mother's funeral . . .' Jerry smouldered for a time, then snapped himself out of that particular resentment. 'It's the fact that there's no ticket for Suzette, his own sister, that's what gets me.'

'Don't worry about me, Jerry,' said Suzette. 'If you're not going, I'm not going.'

So they didn't go. And as I watched the video of this big wedding on Kristen and John Paul's big-screen TV, as I listened to the soundbites of the top table speeches, I couldn't get over a sense of how absurd the whole thing was, the pretence – didn't anybody notice the groom's family was missing? It was like having a funeral without the corpse.

John Paul looked so content, sipping his Texan brew, savouring these highlights of his special day, that I began to suspect the chief reason he wanted me to see all this was not so I could see his passion for Kristen Wingate but so I could witness, retrospectively, concisely, this grand statement of his, this fait accompli. His marriage to one family was a divorce from another.

I wanted to say something, badly, wanted to recognise the absence of the phantoms from this fairy tale, but I knew I couldn't. I was, after all, a guest in the man's house. To my surprise, towards the end of the video, as the bride and groom, now changed into trendy going-away suits, ran the gauntlet of the petal-flinging guests and jumped over dainty brooms, Kristen spoke my mind:

'A pity your father and sister couldn't be there.'

I hardly dared to look over at John Paul. After staring at the retreating limousine and taking a very deliberate sip of beer, he replied, 'Pity Nessa couldn't have been there.'

I stood up. 'Well, thanks for the screening. I don't think I've ever seen a wedding video quite like it.'

I hit the light switch on myself. It was a relief, as if only then the room went dark.

When I came downstairs for breakfast around eight on Monday morning, I found that for the first time John Paul was up before me. Not only that, he was dressed and ready to go. And the way he was dressed stopped me in my tracks – a crisply tailored dark business suit, a dazzlingly white, sharp-collared shirt, and a conservative red-and-green striped tie. He looked as if he was on his way to Richard Nixon's funeral. Kildare Bros. could not have outfitted him more impressively.

This had been mentioned over dinner at the Wingates'. Today Bob was meeting with the people from Detroit, and John Paul was tagging along, as crown prince of the dealership.

'You look a little different this morning,' I said.

'Sideburns,' he said. 'I shaved my sideburns.'

'Ah, that's it.'

'I think he looks like Dan Quayle,' Kristen said. I was beginning to think she could read my mind. She came up behind him and planted a kiss on his baby-smooth cheek. 'But I'd still vote for him.'

John Paul beamed. 'In another two years and eleven months I'll be able to vote for myself.'

'You're planning on taking out citizenship?' I asked.

'Sure.' His brow wrinkled as though I'd asked whether he was planning on breathing three years from now.

'How will that affect your Irish citizenship?' I asked soberly.

He shrugged. 'I have no idea. Coffee?'

An hour later we were in his would-be kingdom. John Paul went up to the bridge to meet the Detroit people; I walked down the front steps of the Temple with a squinting Steve Dildine. The heat immediately began to sizzle the flesh just below my cheek-bones.

'Let's start over here with the Suburbans,' Steve said, pointing to where the rows of scowling vehicles began.

'Oh, no, all Bob wanted me to get was a car, Steve. A Suburban is out of my league.'

The general manager looked up at me, irritation in his squint.

'Well, Bob told *me* you could take anything on the lot.' He slapped my shoulder with sudden levity. 'Except the limited edition Corvettes in the showroom. C'mon, Irish, let's take a look at some SUVs.'

Journeying through the Death Valley of Suburbans, we reached the Tahoes and the Blazers. Steve Dildine's limp was more pronounced today. In the sun his squint had turned to a grimace. I most certainly didn't want the man keeling over on my account, not for a car that I didn't even want in the first place.

'Strikes me that you'd be a Blazer man, just like your buddy,' he said.

Clearly he was trying to sell me on the idea of an SUV, even though he wasn't really selling me anything. I was sorely tempted to give in and take a Blazer (maybe a nice blue one), just to put the man out of his misery and get him back inside to his spreadsheets and his air-conditioning. But I couldn't. I just couldn't. And it was the Irish in me that just couldn't. It wasn't that I distrusted Texans bearing gifts – well, there was an element of that – I just couldn't accept that much.

I said, 'No, I'm sorry, Steve. I don't think any of these SUVs are for me. I'm not sure I'd be able to control one of these machines on the freeway.'

He looked distressed, disappointed. 'You'd be a quick study, I'm sure.'

I shook my head. 'I think I'll just go for a car, an actual car, please.'

He sighed, raised his eyebrows philosophically. Obviously I was no longer an actual man in his eyes.

'Okey-dokey. This way.'

We trekked all the way back across the lot. His limp was getting worse. Making our way through a wide phalanx of pick-up trucks, he turned around and looked at me archly. 'I don't suppose any of these are going to interest you.'

'No,' I replied, looking at the sun-softened tarmac.

He hobbled on, I followed. At last, real cars. Steve seemed as relieved as I was. He leaned against a lamp-post. 'Well, tell you what. Why don't I wait here, catch my breath. You go kick a few tyres and see what takes your fancy.'

I complied. I kicked a few tyres. I let models take my fancy. Cavaliers, Malibus, Luminas – they all looked fine to me. Four-doors, two-doors, convertibles – I would have been happy to test-drive any of them, if there had been any prospect of money changing hands. The compacts I felt a little more comfortable with, the Metros and the Monte Carlos and the Prizms. In fact I must have kicked all four tyres of a two-door Metro, probably because it reminded me of the car of the same name, a Leyland Metro, my mother had driven in the early eighties back home. Steve must have seen me brooding over it because he hobbled over looking very hopeful.

'Found something you like, Irish?'

I was about to say yes, then smiled stickily. 'Well, not really, Steve.'

'Is there a problem with our cars? You don't like Chevys?'

'No, no, it's not that at all, it's just that . . .'

He nodded encouragingly, as if the final truth were about to come out.

'You don't like cars period, right? You think we should have some kind of light rail system like they do back in Europe, right? Some kind of socialised form of transportation.'

He looked like an angry preacher now. I did not want the man having a heart attack out here. Not while I was his customer.

'No, no, I actually like driving, believe it or not. It's just that these cars are all so' – I waved a defeated hand – 'new.'

Dildine looked at me as if I'd suffered brain damage. 'That's right, Irish, these are new cars. You don't want a new car?'

'No.'

'Then why didn't you say so? Let's take a stroll over to pre-owned.'

'Do you mean you have *used* cars?'

'I'll say.'

On the other side of the Temple there was another world of cars, a melting pot – we, at least, were beginning to melt – of makes. Chevys were in the decided majority, especially in the used truck zone, but there were significant minorities of Fords, Toyotas, and Nissans. Dildine grumbled about the number of Korean cars they had on their hands.

'Well, maybe I can help you out there,' I suggested.

He scratched and scoured his beard. 'I don't know about that, Irish. Bob asked me to set up you with something nice. Otherwise I wouldn't have shown you the whole lot.' He gave me a sharp look. 'I don't know about some of these trade-ins. Wouldn't like to see you get burned, son, all the same.'

'But I'm not paying for the car.'

'OK, follow me.'

We kicked about a dozen tyres, imported and American. And I discovered another unfortunate problem. Every car looked as good as new; the sticker prices reflected that evaluation. I was finding it hard to see how I could get away with accepting anything less than four thousand dollars' worth of generosity. Despite what Dildine had said, I just couldn't imagine any of these cars breaking down, even in the desert. They all looked depressingly reliable. Suburban Bob was a man whom you would buy a used car from.

Just at the point where I had lost all hope, and it looked as if Dildine had lost all breath, just at the moment when I was going to give in and take a very sturdy ninety-three Honda Accord, I spied something small and yellow cowering at the end of that row, almost in the grassy ditch at the boundary of the dealership.

'What's that one, at the end?'

Dildine got out of the Accord, which he had been all ready to get the keys for and let me test-drive.

'That. Oh, don't worry about that. It's nothing more than a tin can. Been sitting there for over two years. Korean crap. I've told Marshall to sell it for scrap maybe three times.'

I was already standing over it. It looked like one of those bicycle taxis they have in the Far East. A Hasho Haiku was the make, nine hundred and ninety-nine dollars the asking price. Over the left rear wheel was the first evidence of rust I'd seen in Maverick.

Dildine was huffing his way towards me, limping over the pebbly broken concrete at the border of the lot. He had his hands out as if I were about to break something fragile I'd picked up.

'I'll take it, Mr Dildine.'

He shook his head. 'You can't be serious, Irish. Reagan was in his first term when this thing was built. It doesn't even have any air bags.'

'I've never needed them before.'

'You drive stick?' he asked sceptically.

'Excuse me?'

He mimed a gear change.

I nodded. 'That's what my car back home is.' I put my hand on the thin door handle. 'May I?'

Steve Dildine grunted. 'Knock yourself out.'

When I climbed into the driver's seat – climbed down, I should say – I discovered that the key was right there in the ignition. Had Dildine been hoping someone would just come along and steal it? If so, I hoped I could be of service.

The first two times I tried to start the car, terrible sounds came from the engine, as if someone were drilling rivets into it. In the side-view mirror I could see Dildine hobbling closer, a hot smirk on his small face. I tried the key for a third, determined time – and the Haiku started up like a lawnmower. But my delight was delayed by the shock of the automatic seat belt, which almost garrotted me as it swung into place. I released myself from it so that I could speak in an unfettered way to Steve Dildine. After rolling down the window I nodded vigorously and delivered my verdict: 'The Haiku is mine.'

There were no appeals.

I waited around the now quiet showroom until Bob and John Paul came back from their meeting with the Detroit people, which had extended into lunch at a restaurant called Café Sidney; apparently a very big Maverick deal. Bob was in his usual how-the-hell-are-you mood, but I suspected this was a bit of a brave face: he had looked startlingly subdued as I'd caught sight of him and his son-in-law coming up the steps of the Temple. John Paul continued to be subdued inside. I did not ask how things had gone, but my mind was busy with speculation. Had the Detroit people examined the prince and found him wanting? Could the corporation veto a dealership succession? If there was something rotten in the state of Wingate Chevy, was Truck Nation still waiting in the wings, itching to take over? These questions would have to wait; for now it was my duty to answer.

'Steve fix you up all right carwise?' Bob asked.

'Absolutely.'

'What you go for in the end?'

I told him the make. It sounded as if I was clearing my throat.

'Excuse me?' Bob said.

A smile was wriggling its way onto John Paul's face.

'Haiku, Bob. I went for the Haiku.'

He looked at me for a moment uncomprehendingly, then exploded with laughter.

'Good one,' he said, slapping me so hard on the shoulder that I was afraid I would be left with a bruise. 'Enjoy, whatever it is.' He walked past me. 'I've got some calls to make. You boys take care now.'

I was facing John Paul. He said:

'I think perhaps you'd better follow me at close quarters on the freeway.'

'Do we have to take the freeway?'

He looked at me as if I'd asked if we had to eat today.

As I made my solo debut on the Splendora Freeway, the opening line of a novel I'd started in college – don't ask me the title – came back to me. Something about people in Los Angeles being afraid to merge on freeways. Well, in Maverick no one was afraid to merge on freeways. It was second nature. They lived to merge on freeways, found it bracing and good for the soul – especially when there was no acceleration lane, which, according to a diamond-shaped sign on the feeder road, was the attraction of the entry ramp John Paul chose for us. The Blazer merged snugly, without hesitation, as if the hammering traffic were waiting with a soft embrace.

No such luck for me. The Haiku's sideview mirror proving insufficient – it gave me a very nice view of the sky and a few SUV roofs – I had to crane my neck back over a bleak concrete parapet, taking my eyes so completely of the road ahead that my left tyres pummelled over knobbily side markings. But looking back at least allowed me to see that merging at that moment, my moment, would have amounted to a shameless death wish. Packed traffic was charging down all five lanes. Perhaps I should just have rolled onto the shoulder at that point, strewn as it was with slivery pieces of metal and snaky strips of old tyre, but instead I stopped right on the cusp on the nearest lane. A Land Rover braked hard behind me.

Driving on the feeder road had alerted me to the Haiku's puny rate of acceleration; the whining engine appeared to have been transferred from the body of a radio-contolled model aeroplane. That meant that I dared not merge until there was a generous break in the traffic.

But I-29 was not in a generous mood. And so an impressive line of vehicles built up behind me. I avoided looking in the rearview mirror as much as possible – Americans can say such much with their fingers – but the honking and blasting was harder to ignore. Soon I understood: the other drivers didn't really care if it was risky for me to merge; they just wanted me to move. If they could have, I'm sure they would have flung me into the middle of the action as a sacrifice to Maverick's hot gods.

In the end, I decided to sacrifice myself. There was an arguable break in the stream of vehicles coming up beside me and the next car was a mere compact – better to have a collision of equals. I put the pedal to the floor (it didn't have far to travel) and went for it. The oncoming car braked violently – a useful overreaction. But judging from the horn war that erupted for some distance down the lane, I almost caused, indirectly, a Texas-sized pile-up.

Then again, I had just lost my merging virginity. But John Paul, my freeway coach, was nowhere to be seen. Yet if I could merge without an acceleration lane, surely I could do anything. I would find New Plantation myself. I had a good recollection of the route we'd taken from the airport last week. So I forged ahead. And apart from an eighteen-wheeler roaring by, almost buffeting the Haiku into the rubbish-strewn shoulder, things went smoothly for a time. Not that I did anything extreme like attempt a lane change, but I did feel that I was at least in control of where I was going. I didn't need John Paul's guidance.

Suddenly there he was – *behind* me, flashing his headlights, closing fast. For a moment I thought the Blazer was going to rear-end me. I tried to shift the Haiku into the highest of its limited repertoire of gears, but that turned out to involve a complex manoeuvre whereby you had to go down a gear before you could advance by two. By the time I had completed this Zen mechanism, the Blazer was gone from my rearview mirror. Then it was conspicuous again, engaged in an arc of lane changes that brought John Paul right in front of me, where he was meant to be in the first place. I slowed down – one thing the Haiku could do with ease – and trailed him at a respectable distance. After that, no more stunts, from him or from me.

Back at Pocahontas Lane, John Paul insisted that I park in the garage, beside the Camero; he left the Blazer on the road. I suspected this arrangement was motivated more by embarrassment than courtesy. In any case, I put the Haiku under cover, content to be parked next to Kristen.

John Paul and I met back out on the sweltering driveway.

I said, 'Bit of a scare you gave me back there.'

Amused, he replied, 'Bit of a scare you gave yourself.'

If this were Dublin, I thought, I might just throw a pint in your face.

I shrugged and said mildly, 'Anyway I survived.'

My attitude pleased him. 'I think you'd make it here in Maverick, Peter Dagg. You're a sharp guy, in your own way.'

'That I am,' I replied. 'That I am. Shall we go inside and join Kristen?'

That night we played pool in the games room.

In most of the frames John Paul played, either against me or

Kristen, he cleared the table with furious accuracy. Once, as he lined up his cue behind a sweetly placed eight ball – most of my solids were still scattered on the felt – he said, 'The Detroit people are going to be in town for another day. Want to hang out with the visiting Irishman tomorrow, Kris?'

Kristen, sitting slimly on a stool, sipped her wine cooler and replied, 'Which one?'

Her husband looked up from the shot he was sighting, gave her a sour smile, then turned back and hammered the black home.

The next morning I didn't even get to see John Paul in his suit; he was gone before I woke up. But it was decidedly pleasant to breakfast exclusively with Kristen, who had indeed kindly agreed to give over her day off to chaperoning the (officially) visiting Irishman. She made a pot of tea from the Bewley's bags she'd ordered for John Paul over the internet.

'So what are we going to do with ourselves?' I asked.

'In a word?'

'In a word.'

'Shop.'

I nodded sincerely. 'Great idea. I need to find something for Suzette.'

When she said shop, I assumed she meant we'd be going to Rustic Mall, but no, Kristen's idea was to give me what she called, with only a light coat of irony, Maverick's premier shopping experience, The Global Village.

So, on another atomically hot but abundantly blue Texas morning, we took the now familiar route along the Splendora freeway to the Beltway. This was a much more enjoyable ride. Not only had we missed the worst of the rush hour traffic – this was the Platonic ideal of freeway travel compared to my first experience on I-29 – but after John Paul, Kristen's driving was so sensible, so mature. Now I understood that travelling around Maverick did not have to be an extreme sport. I made a joking reference to her taking in the rules of the road with her mother's milk, which, in the intimacy of her Camero, then made me fear I was blushing. Kristen took it in her stride. Kristen looked as if she could take anything in her stride. She was married to John Paul Mountain, after all. The station of choice on her radio was heavy on introspective female rock.

'Not a country fan like your husband?'

Her eyes momentarily rolled up and away from the road.

'Oh, country I like' – she gave me a sharp, pastiche-sexy glance – 'but I don't make as big a deal out of it as John Paul, him and his phases.'

Oh, we knew all about John Paul and his phases back in Dublin.

'What, you mean he's gone through a polka phase or something also?'

She smiled politely. 'No, but there was this AM station he listened to all last summer, RightTalk.'

'Sounds dreadful.'

'It is. Even the gardening advice show has a conservative slant.'

Funny, yes, but not as funny as my long, hearty laugh suggested.

I had intended to bring up the subject of the wedding – softly, softly style – but Kristen did that for me before we reached the Beltway. It started with a simple question about the reception, then developed into a detailed interrogation about Daire's cuisine and the politics of getting married in the Church. (At one point Jerry had threatened not to come because of that alleged last straw, but we'd called his bluff, knowing he couldn't bear missing both of his children's weddings. He was not the apostate he had once been.)

At first I found all the wedding talk gratifying, but then, as we sped towards the blue-grey profile of the Consort Tower, I grew frustrated. There was an air of unreality here, because Kristen was acting as if she would be there, in Dublin in person, as if she were going to be an integral part of Suzette and Peter's Big Day, a member of the wedding party. To hear her carry on, you'd swear her husband was going to be my best man.

There was a break in the wedding cross-examination while Kristen made her no-fuss, no-drama exit from the Beltway.

I said, 'You know, I think that Consort Tower is actually quite attractive. That kind of architecture makes sense in a place like this.'

Kristen smiled, threw me a shrewd look, flirted with me out of the corner of her eye.

'That's nice of you to say so, Peter, but that's not the Consort Tower.'

'John Paul said it was.'

'John Paul doesn't know what he's talking about. They changed the name last week. Now it's the Gastec Tower. You're looking at the Gastec Tower.'

'Under new management?'

'To the tune of one billion dollars. Here if you buy the building, you buy the name.'

'But won't the good people of Maverick just keeping on using the old name? It has a bit of poetry about it.'

Kristen shook her head. 'Not for long.' And smiled again. 'I've already made the change.'

On Cadwallader Boulevard we stopped at a red left-turn light. Behind a chi-chi shopping centre, featuring jewellery shops and furriers, rose a blue sphere gilded with the continents. It was perched on top of a giant white mausoleum; inside that tomb we would find The Global Village.

Kristen had started in on our honeymoon (it was to be a French wine-tasting odyssey). An elderly Hispanic man wearing a white suit with a red martial stripe was walking up and down the concrete strip, his face a cataract of sweat, his smile plump and permanent. The large collection can he was holding read, LA LUZ DEL MONDO. As far as I could see, he didn't get a penny from the line of cars.

Instead of answering Kristen's latest question (was I buying or renting my tuxedo), I replied by saying, 'Kristen,' – diplomatic sigh – 'let me ask you something, if I may.' Did she tense her hands around the steering wheel? I went on: 'Why don't you come? We'd love so much for you to be there . . . both of you.'

She smiled. What kind of smile it was I wasn't sure – relief? irritation? – because she was wearing those mandatory Maverick driving shades, not as impenetrable as her husband's, but still a barrier. Then she got the green light and I had to wait for a reply until careful Kristen had made the tight turn.

'Peter, I don't know how to even begin answering that question.'

'Try, please.'

'It's the question I've been avoiding and obsessing about all this time. I guess you picked up on that.'

'Please try.'

She sighed forcefully. Who was she frustrated with, most? She spoke briskly. 'I'd go in a heartbeat – that you know. I want to go because I think it would be good for John Paul. But also' – she looked right and left going through a busy intersection – 'I think it would be good for me.'

Half a block later I asked, 'How so?'

Instead of answering she turned right and drove up the ramp of a parking garage cowering beneath the mausoleum. At the barrier she took off her shades and wound down the whiny automatic window. Before taking the fat ticket the machine trundled out, she turned to me, her eyes looking raw in the orange murk, and said, with a stiff smile, 'Let's talk about this later, Peter. A little shopping and I'll be ready for anything.'

*   *   *

The Global Village was another master-planned community. Each arcade was modelled and named after an international street that had proved to be a hit with American tourists; now they could shop the world in climate-controlled safety. The simulated streets had their own replica signs and façades, behind which were, more often than not, familiar domestic retailers.

So – we began our tour, hunting for leather luggage under the iron arches of the Passage de l'Opéra; laughing at the garish fashions on Carnaby Street; wandering from one end of St Mark's Square to the other; admiring the porcelain of Parizska Street; getting into our stride along Kurfürstendamm; eating ice cream as we strolled down the Rambla; crossing the Rialto into Orchard Road; getting squirted with perfumes as we wound our way through the Khan el Khalili Bazaar; losing each other in the Marrakesh Casbah; trying on sunglasses in the simulated night-glow of the Temple Street Market; and, finally, finding ourselves back at the foot of the Spanish Steps for a much-needed espresso.

'Well,' I said, 'I saw an Irish pub, but no Grafton Street.'

Kristen laughed listlessly. 'If there were a Grafton Street he'd be here every day. As it is, he's fond enough of that McCourt's.'

I felt I could, and should, speak bluntly now.

'Is that where his lost weekends start?'

Kristen ripped open a sachet of sugar imprinted with the profiles of Keats and Shelley, that read, in Gothic print, Caffè Roma. She sipped her water and smiled, but not sweetly. 'I remember asking him, just after we'd arrived here and were staying over at my mom's house, what my parents should say. And you know what his answer was? "Tell them to tell their friends my family is dead."' Kristen shook her head mournfully, then perked up again:

'He wasn't quite as brutal, though, when it came to the invitations. Kept on saying, "Let me think about it." Mom started to put him under some subtle pressure. He was getting on so well with my parents – this unremitting charm offensive on all other fronts – that in the end he gave in and sent the big invitations.'

'But no plane tickets.'

She flinched, then stared. 'No plane tickets? Yes, there were plane tickets. Dad made sure that everybody coming from Ireland would be able to get here.' Those chameleon eyes narrowed. 'What do you know, Peter?'

I sighed. 'Perhaps you'd better ask John Paul about that. No, you should definitely ask *him* about that.'

But she wasn't listening. 'You bastard,' she muttered, staring at the marble table top. 'You fake.'

It had all begun so well, she said. Perfectly. Magically. He had been so creative, so considerate. It was John Paul's idea to make the honeymoon into an extended pilgrimage to all the places that had a hallowed connection with her subject, Singer Sargent.

They travelled for two months. After warming up in London and Paris (so close to Dublin, so far), they went to the Tyrolean Mountains, to Venice, to Spain, to the Moroccan town of Tétouan. And then – she hesitated.

'And then?'

'And then we came back to the States,' she replied, down-mouthed. 'To Boston.'

'What happened in Boston?'

I felt as if I were prodding a reluctant prosecution witness.

Kristen frowned. 'While I went to study Singer Sargent's murals at the Museum of Fine Arts, my husband toured the Irish bars of the Combat Zone.' She shrugged. 'And that was the end of the honeymoon.'

I said, softly, 'But isn't that in the nature of a honeymoon, Kristen?'

She looked up. 'Is it in the nature of a marriage to find out you've

113

married a stranger? Or in my case, two strangers – master-planned-community John Paul and absent-without-leave John Paul?'

I looked at the rectangular ceramic holder packed tight with sachets of pseudo-Roman sugar.

'Two strangers,' I nodded. 'Yes. Yes indeed. That's John Paul, all right.'

The first place we went into, post-coffee, had little more decor than a parquet floor and a single rack of scrappy dresses, the clothes almost outnumbered by sullen young women posing as sales 'associates'. But I had no right to be critical. Dublin was getting like that too. Selling less for more. We couldn't get enough of it.

Kristen sidled up beside me.

'See anything here for your beloved?'

I had to think fast. 'Yes. But nothing very Suzette. And I don't want to settle for anything less.'

Kristen nodded at my wisdom. 'I understand.'

At the shoe shop next door, she fell in love with something for herself: a pair of flat-toed black sandals with a swath of zebra hide.

'Do you approve?' she asked, her foot coyly turning on its dainty, painted big toe.

'I do, I do,' I reply, knowing full well that they were going to be hers whether I approved or not.

I eyed the credit card receipt as she signed it: a hundred and ninety-five dollars. I would have to deliver two leaves-for-appeal to cover that. I would have delivered a dozen.

That night we ate Cajun take-away.

All John Paul wanted to talk about was the latest Texas execution, showing off in the process his knowledge of the appeals process and the protocols of the Department of Corrections. At last Kristen changed the subject to what had been the big story on the Channel

7 news, the giant smoke cloud heading Maverick's way. Apparently, this was an annual hazard, Maverick's dense mistral. Thousands of impoverished Central American farmers were clearing their fields with fire. The fruits of their labour would reach the city by the weekend.

'It was bad enough last year,' she said. 'Lord knows what it's going to be like this year.'

'It'll be OK,' John Paul replied, scalping another crayfish. 'It's mostly hype, Pete. Just smells like somebody's barbecuing slightly rancid meat in the neighbourhood.'

'What a relief,' I said.

'We could get out of town for a few days,' Kristen suggested forcefully. 'Show Peter the Hill Country.' She gave me a Mona Lisa smile. 'I'm sure you'll find something for Suzette in Winter's Mill. It a shopper's paradise.'

Why did the prospect of paradise make me feel shy?

'But what about your work?' I asked, looking from one to the other.

John Paul shook his head. 'Bob won't have a problem with me going out of town for a few days right now.'

Things, I gathered, hadn't gone any better with the people from Detroit.

'Good then, that's settled,' Kristen said. 'I'll phone the Lightfoot Inn.'

The name stimulated John Paul, but he cautioned, 'Don't you think it's going to be hard to book at such short notice?'

Kristen shook her head. 'I'll phone Eleanor and get it all sorted out. There'll be room for you, dear, don't worry.'

John Paul looked at me archly. 'You see, Peter. She's her father's daughter. Always drives a hard bargain, does Kristen Wingate-Mountain.'

The three days between the smoke cloud alert and our departure for the Hill Country I spent largely by myself. Kristen and John Paul had to put in long hours at the dealership to justify (to themselves more than Bob, I suspected) taking off for the weekend, though I wondered how much work John Paul actually got done sitting in his Sales Coordinator office.

So both of them officially had their jobs to do, and I – I had my Haiku. The three of us would have a large, early breakfast (quite the ménage we were becoming) and reconvene, after the dealership had closed, at some popular ethnic restaurant for a large, late dinner. Thai, Persian, Ethiopian – we ate the world.

These interlude days should have been the dullest I spent in Maverick, but I think of them as the richest. And I am not talking about the gargantuan meals that started and ended the day. Between meals came the very rich hours. In my less-than-trusty Haiku, which often issued creaky rumours of its demise but never quite conked out, I discovered Maverick for myself. Kristen had equipped me with a map and a mobile. The map I used often – folding and crumpling it desperately at mystery intersections – the phone, never. I might have been lost, but I didn't want help. Being lost wasn't so bad, I discovered.

When I told John Paul and Kristen over dinner about some of the places I'd found myself in that particular day, their jaws would sag before the laughter began. You went *where*? You drove all the way out *there*?

I did. A sample itinerary:

South of Logan Hollow, I crossed the tracks, or a ridge of earth where tracks had once stretched, and entered an unincorporated area called Summertown. I crossed those ghost tracks, and the language of the landscape changed. Businesses formed a rhythm – *taqueria, panadería, carnicería, taqueria.* On the street (Tyburn it was called and, according to the Haiku's jerky milometer, it lasted four miles) there were many more people to be seen than back in Logan Hollow, and here the faces were all bronzed. I passed small body shops, convenience stores with barred windows, and shopping subcentres with pebble-dash façades featuring pawnshops, cheque-cashing operations, and nail salons; more nail salons than food stores.

Between the commercial strips were brown apartment complexes with roofs slanting every which way, and names that sounded like master-planned communities: Oxford Park, Berkeley Forest, Napoleon Oaks. But the wood of these buildings looked weathered more by age than design.

Then for two blocks I drove through a virtual fiesta as I passed used-car lot after used-car lot, each dealership trying to outdo its neighbours with festoons of small fluttering flags. The only thing to spoil the festive spirit were the actual cars themselves, many of them close relations and peers of my Haiku.

But my best find came towards the end of Tyburn. Between a *taqueria* and a washeteria stood a white barn with a big red-painted sign that read, LA LUZ DEL MONDO. I recalled the afternoon Kristen had driven me to Global Village, and wished now, irrationally I knew, that I'd rolled down my window and given the man in the white military suit a dollar or two.

Tyburn ended at a T-junction, across which there was a wasteland of patchy grass and, in the extreme distance, an elevated portion of a freeway I could not identify. Both ways of the junction led, as far as I could see, nowhere in particular. I turned nowhere left.

On Friday I phoned Suzette. Outside the guest bedroom window there was a subtle haze. If hadn't known about the illegal-alien cloud I would have assumed it was an odd summer fog, which in a sense I suppose it was.

'I'm leaving Maverick,' I told my fiancée after the usual sweet greetings.

'Mission accomplished?' she asked with a rare excitement in her voice.

'No, sorry, I mean I'm leaving Maverick, not Texas. Just for a few days. The weather's not great here. We're going to the Hill Country.'

'You mean you're leaving with *them*.'

I sighed, such a mature sigh. 'Suzette, what are you driving at? I thought you trusted my judgment. And if my judgment tells me that I might get around to the essential business of my trip – which I have not lost sight of for one minute, by the way – in the more conducive surroundings of this Hill Country, why should you question that? It's just a holiday, dear.'

A static-free pause, then she replied, 'Peter, sweetie, you're already on holiday.'

I let my exasperation show in an acidic sigh. 'I'll be back on Monday.'

Though we left New Plantation at three o'clock, we still got caught in the end-of-week traffic snarl once we hit the Beltway. It was an hour before we were clear of Maverick and its mess of signs. The NorthTex Freeway took us in its eponymous direction. John Paul, driving, was in fine form once he was able to go over the speed limit – seventy on the open road, beyond the city limits.

I was sitting up front beside him. Occasionally Kristen would remind him of speed traps near small towns; he had been caught the last time they had gone to Hill Country and had been given a ticket, his first – and allegedly his only – brush with American law. He told me he had taken something called Defensive Driving to expunge the ticket from his record. Whatever that course had involved, it had left not a trace upon his driving style. John Paul's driving was all offensive.

At first the landscape was exactly what I had seen in the unde-veloped areas on the way to New Plantation – rigorously flat and adorned only with scrubby oak and the occasional pine forest. But after another hour the land began to roll and real farmland was visible on either side of the slimmer freeway.

We passed the white wooden gateways of ranches, with their brand-letter insignia and their dirt avenues winding lazily to houses sheltered by thicker oaks. Service strips indicated small towns whose hearts we couldn't see, though at least twice John Paul almost breezed onto the commercial loops that would have taken us there. Kristen seemed to appreciate his last nanosecond lane changes as much as I did.

The land began to divide itself into definite hills.

'If this is the real Texas, I like it,' I said.

'You mean you don't like Maverick,' John Paul deadpanned.

'No, no,' I replied slowly, 'I like Maverick. But I like this more.'

At my shoulder Kristen said, 'Peter, you haven't seen anything yet.'

As the light began to fade we left the freeway and took a road called FM – Farm and Market – 296. We extracted some light irony from the coincidence that now the HipCountry 102 FM signal began to scratch and shudder, fading more every time we dipped into another little valley. That more than anything put me in a holiday mood. By now I knew the station's playlist off by heart. Three times since leaving New Plantation we'd heard John Paul's current favourite: the new one from Rusty Steets, in which each magnet on a 'frigerator' door became the inspiration for a verse dedicated to a particular time and place in the singer's life.

Once we lost the signal completely, I thought John Paul would simply tune to a more local country station – there had to be a handful – but he demurred.

'The kind of country they play up here is a little too country for my taste,' he explained shyly.

Kristen made a mock-superior nasal sound, or perhaps it wasn't so mock. 'You see, Peter, my husband is just a suburban boy with cowboy boots.'

I made sure to laugh. In reality I was reflecting that I still found it stranger to think of John Paul as a suburbanite than a cowboy.

As darkness fell, Kristen granted that we were in real Hill Country. The road wound between ever-higher terraces of rock and rough greenery.

At last we went through the heart of a bona fide town, Mason, its bright Victorian main street perched high on a hill, reminding me of San Francisco, where I had never been, but where I had originally planned to be by now.

Kristen and John Paul were united on one point: that it would be a crime not to take a detour and go eat at The Big Pit, a legendary barbecue place off the beaten track.

'People come from as far as Austin and San Antonio to eat there,' Kristen told me.

John Paul turned to me and asked, 'Y'interested?'

'I'm up for any adventure,' I told them, thinking, I really am.

There was an immediate benefit in deciding to find this mythic restaurant: just outside Mason, Kristen took over the wheel. John Paul had slowed down a little since we'd reached the hills and night had fallen, but not enough for my liking. But they had been to The Big Pit only once before and John Paul had to admit that he wasn't quite sure how to find it. So, with Kristen in control, we turned off the farm road onto an even narrower and darker route.

Soon I had completely lost my bearings, the segment of winding road revealed by the Blazer's headlights my only point of reference. We could have been driving underground. My thoughts wandered, as they might have in a sensory deprivation chamber. I remembered being driven, in the same pure darkness, on the back roads of West Cork, in the remote seventies of my childhood, coming back from the farmhouse of one of my mother's cousins – swimming in that darkness, my father dipping the headlights of his Leyland

Princess the rare times we met another vehicle on those thin and slithering roads.

But I was never afraid, unbuckled in the back seat. I had an absolute, unreflective confidence in my father's driving. How different John Paul and Suzette's holidays must have been, in the same county, down in the fashionable enclave of Kinsale.

Aswim in the pitch black of Texas, I felt almost as safe with Kristen Wingate driving. She had the same solidity as my parents. She made danger distant, in the way that John Paul's driving made it intimate. She would find this place, no matter how convoluted the way. Kristen was one of us. She would get us there safely.

And she did.

The eponymous open-pit barbecue was the size of a tennis court. After consuming many pounds of savoury, smoky cow and every other hoofed and feathered beast, we continued on our way to the Lightfoot Inn, Kristen once again driving and navigating, with limited assistance from myself struggling with the regional map, a filigree of rural roads running through the purple bruises of the Hill Country. A few times even Kristen thought we'd taken the wrong turn. The last time she and John Paul had arrived at the bed-and-breakfast it hadn't been dark, and they hadn't been coming from the obscure direction of The Big Pit.

But at last, towards nine o'clock, six hours after we'd set out from New Plantation, and after driving along a final, deserted, hill-hugging road for a dozen miles or more, the Blazer's headlights caught a wooden sign telling us the turn for the Lightfoot Inn was just another quarter-mile ahead.

My sense of relief was spoiled by the nerve-racking ride up the flinty, steep road, serpentine and walled in by thick forest – we endured at least a half-mile of that, the Blazer rocking from side to side.

Hanging onto the window grip, I said, 'I wonder if a conventional car could even make it up this road.'

'Ah,' said John Paul, 'we have a convert, a ute convert.'

We clawed our way around one more dramatic corner and drove into a small gravelled compound. It was dominated by a two-storey wood house with a double porch facing out into the black woods. Nearby was a long bungalow. The main house was bright with inviting lights. Suddenly I was very pleased to be here.

'There she is,' Kristen said. 'There's Eleanor.'

A silhouette had appeared at the side door. We stepped down onto the gravel with our light weekend luggage. My eyes were drawn up to the dome of sharp stars. There had been no night sky like this above New Plantation. A ghost of a cloud momentarily veiled a fat star. In Texas even the clouds moved faster than back home, as if they had the benefit of celestial freeways. Back on earth Kristen and John Paul were holding hands, tentatively, as we crunched our way towards the house.

The woman of the house was wearing an old jacket over a simple print dress on this hot night (hot but somehow a different hot to the nocturnal Maverick heat). She had cropped auburn hair and a sternly attractive face. Her smile was welcoming, but with an element of intelligent reserve. If I'd been told she was thirty-five or forty-five I would have accepted it. She looked like a beauty who had allowed her looks to become weathered, or had actively encouraged that weathering, up here in the Hill Country.

For all her understatement, her coolness – or maybe because of it – something about her pulsed Woman with a Past, Woman with a Past. I doubted she had been born in these parts.

'Good to have you back,' Eleanor said to Kristen and John Paul.

But did I catch the flick of a wry smile in the unreliable light?

John Paul said, 'Eleanor, this is our friend Peter.'

Nothing about Ireland. Did she even know that John Paul was

Irish? I knew he would never have volunteered the information. (Though I wonder if she had figured out in any case. There was something intuitive, subtle, *Canadian* about her.) But why did I care so much that he didn't tell strangers where he was from originally? Perhaps I just needed Ireland more than he did.

I shook her hand and noted her long concert-pianist fingers.

'Welcome to the Lightfoot Inn,' she said. 'You'll be in the Half-Moon suite, next door to the Wingates.'

'Excellent,' I replied.

We followed Eleanor inside to a spacious kitchen. The walls above the counters were dense with brassy utensils. The room was dominated by a round table whose raw wooden surface was at least six feet in diameter. This was my kind of kitchen.

Eleanor said, 'That's where we have breakfast – everybody together about eight-thirty.'

John Paul and Kristen got positively gushy.

'The breakfast *is* phenomenal, Peter,' she said.

'Eleanor, you simply have to start marketing that muesli of yours,' he said.

The chatelaine of the Lightfoot Inn didn't pay too much attention to this flattery. Instead, for my benefit, she led us on a quick tour of the rest of the house.

Any guest could use the broad porch on the ground floor; the slightly narrower one on the upper floor was exclusively ours. Downstairs was rigorously clean, the wooden interiors giving it a Scandinavian feel. The living room was decorated with Indian art and artefacts, lovingly collected, I sensed. The small library was, from the cursory glance I got of it, exclusively devoted to titles concerning Native American culture – mythology, history, belief.

Kristen was excited to see the tiny rough-hewn arrowhead she had found near the house on their previous visit, now mounted in a small glass box on the wall.

Eleanor told me, 'In seven years only three guests have found arrowheads – and your friends were the only people to donate theirs to the house collection.'

No wonder she was willing to do Kristen a favour.

John Paul nodded righteously. 'It stays where it belongs.'

The downstairs bedrooms, Eleanor explained, had been taken by two couples from Houston. They would be staying the weekend also. Eleanor herself lived in the smaller house.

We followed her up the solid wooden stairs, our way punctuated with more Apache artefacts on the bare wood wall.

We had the top floor to ourselves. Besides our bedrooms, there was a large bathroom, a communal area softened with Navajo throw-rugs, and the soothing porch.

Both rooms were doubles, but John Paul and Kristen's Ghost Dance was the larger of the two. Half-Moon was not luxurious but eminently comfortable, the kind of room where you wouldn't mind spending a winter, if you had to spend a winter indoors – preferably with a cosy partner.

'What's that, may I ask?' I said to Eleanor, pointing to a curiosity hanging above my bed: a furry circle webbed with black string and daubed with little coloured feathers.

'That?' she replied. 'That's a dreamcatcher. Never seen one before?' It was as if I didn't know what a crucifix was.

'No,' I said, making nice. 'But I'm glad it's there, I suppose.'

Eleanor smiled. 'Well, I'll just go and see if the Wingates have everything they need. See you in the morning, Peter. Pleasant dreams.' She half winked. 'The dreamcatcher filters out your night-mares, you know.'

I had this whimsical image of Eleanor's bed, in her own private cabin, surrounded by those dreamcatchers.

If these things work, I thought, they should get one to hang over John Paul's head in New Plantation. Perhaps then he could at least get to sleep.

When I came out of Half-Moon, the Wingates were lounging in our living room.

John Paul nodded at my feet. 'I hope those are your dancing shoes, Peter.'

'Sure.' I was wearing a casual but sensible pair of Clark's – my standard footwear for the trip. 'Why do you ask?'

He smiled. 'Because Kristen here is going to teach you how to two-step.'

She smiled and nodded in agreement.

I shrugged. 'Well, I'm up for anything. But where are we going to try this? Is there a stereo or something up here?'

'Hell, no,' John Paul replied. 'We're going to bring you to the best boot scootin' insti-tootion in the Hill Country.'

Kristen raised her eyes in happy exasperation.

'And where would that be, John Paul?' I asked.

'Bum's.'

'Bum's?'

'Yep. Place on the other side of Frankfurt.'

'Isn't that one of the towns we passed . . . ages ago?'

'Correct, sir.'

Kristen said, 'My husband has another motivation for going there.'

'And what would that be?'

A tight smile from John Paul.

'This is a dry county, my friend. And Bum's is just over the county line.'

So we took another mystery ride in the Blazer, this one lasting at least half an hour.

All the way I felt scandalised that there could still be any zone of the United States where, on both a *de jure* and a *de facto* basis, a grown-up person could not buy a drink. It was simply . . . un-American. (It was definitely un-Irish.)

No sooner had the Blazer's headlights illuminated the green sign welcoming us to Barton County than Bum's, that bastion of freedom, came into view on our left, a long, deep shack with a bold red neon sign.

Now it was the Blazer's turn to be in the minority as Kristen parked in a large dusty lot thick with pick-up trucks. On the front steps we were met by a rotund young man in a black cowboy hat and boot-cut jeans who was nominally a bouncer but who greeted us like long-lost relatives; he became a little emotional when I tried to reach for age-ascertaining ID.

Inside the cowboy hats were so dense that they formed a kind of eye-level marquee. Many of the women – achingly good-looking, most of them – wore them, too; everyone wore jeans. Thank God I had changed into a pair before we left. Hatless, I felt wimpish enough, sure that we were going to look horribly out of place and get suspicious looks from local men just bristling for a fight on a Friday night.

But the clientele of Bum's were a lot more relaxed than I was. Most of the place was taken up by a crowded dance floor, with high tables on one side and a long bar on the other. Beer paraphernalia was the extent of the decoration – strings of little pendants hung between posts, neon logos around the bar, sharp in the murky light. In one corner a whiskery DJ was playing steel-guitar country tunes that were mercifully light on lyrics.

Between numbers his voice boomed out of the PA. I couldn't distinguish one word he said from the other, but the crowd, most notably John Paul, cheered his interjections. A few feet into the place we'd been confronted by a beautiful girl with buck teeth wearing only a bikini top above her beltless jeans. She was standing behind a raw metal bucket the size of a small bathtub brimming with ice and embedded bottles of the evening's featured beer.

John Paul bought three bottles, bantering with the beer girl as she wrapped them with napkins. Kristen stared at the dance floor. I spoke up above the music.

'So, Kristen, is this the real Texas?'

'Oh, real enough.'

Her husband handed us a bottle each. We followed him to one of the high tables. There was one stool. John Paul took it.

'So, you gonna teach our friend how to two-step?' he said to Kristen.

She took a sip from her beer and put it down. 'Sure.'

I said, 'Don't we get to be wallflowers for a little while?'

She smiled and took me by the hand. 'Don't know what you're talking about.' I put down my beer and followed her.

'I must warn you,' I said as we squeezed our way out onto the floor. 'I'm a bit of a dance illiterate. Suzette claims I have two left feet. She's very worried I'll mess things up when we have to lead off the waltz at the wedding reception.'

Kristen stopped me and put her arms lightly on my shoulders. Looking up she said, 'Perhaps when I send you back she'll notice the difference.'

I looked down at our opposing feet. She was wearing those zebra sandals.

'Just mimic me,' she said.

'I'll try.'

I would have been less intimidated by the prospect of committing a thousand statuary instruments to memory.

At first I just couldn't get it. It was like trying to waltz to a regular beat. I kept missing a step, or putting an extra step in. Twice our feet became tangled. I lost count of the number of times I stepped on her toes; I'm sure she didn't. But every time she was gracious about it, forgiving, patient as a real teacher should be.

One time I crushed her little toe, but even then her wince turned into a smile. I shuddered to think what permanent damage I would have done had I been wearing a pair of boots, like every other man on that floor.

Finally she said, 'Don't think about it so much. Just let go. Focus on the music.'

I know in films that's when the metamorphosis takes place; that's when the ugly duckling dancer turns into a flashdancing swan. For about a half a minute it worked. We began to twirl around the dance floor with something approaching simultaneous grace. If there hadn't been other couples on the floor perhaps we would have continued to cruise smoothly.

But there were other couples, and I reversed disastrously into the broad back of a giant cowboy. His partner was almost as tall and she gave me a filthy look. I wanted to pack up there and then, but Kristen put her arms back on my shoulders, looked into my eyes (this close, her eyes indisputably blue), and said, 'Don't give up now. You've almost got it.'

What I really wanted at that moment was four or five beers to blur my embarrassment, but when she looked into my eyes and said that, what else could I do but follow her instruction?

So we started into the two-step once again, and this time I kept time methodically.

It went better, much better; by the end of that twangy number I was doing what I was meant to do – leading. Suddenly I wanted to two-step all night.

But then the lights on the floor dimmed even further, the upbeat music came to an end, and the DJ said something loud and slurred and significant. Suddenly Bum's dance floor could have been Old Berchmans Rugby Football Club teen disco with the opening soppy strains of 'Knights in White Satin' wafting from the amplifiers, instead of this plodding song about some good ol' boy navel gazing. The slow set had begun.

Couples began to peel away from the dance floor, and were very slow to be replenished.

I said, 'Let's see how John Paul is getting on.'

She nodded, a little reluctantly, I judged.

When he saw us, he put down the drink in his hand – a *drink* drink, straight whiskey – and grinned.

'Well, you two make a cute couple.'

The next morning I woke up early. Seven-fifteen, according to my solid watch.

I stepped out onto the porch, and saw for the first time the full wonder of the place I'd been brought to: undulating trees as far as the eye could see, broken only by the occasional terraced rockery of a hilltop; the faultline of a lonely road; and on the horizon, on the lip of a valley, a hint of the outskirts of Winter's Mill.

A bird of prey – let's call it a hawk – was gliding against the light blue sky. Though it was impossibly high up, I could still make out the sharp teeth of the feathers along the back of its wings.

I was in a different state. Kristen was right: I had seen nothing yet. I sat down in the warm shade, in a big rocking chair. It was warm, agreeably warm.

Above the wooden balustrade a blue-green hummingbird appeared, its buzzing and blurred wings making it appear more insect than bird – a fat bee. It hovered near a water dispenser suspended from the eave, its needle-beak occasionally tapping the little red plastic reservoir at the base.

I took soft steps as close to the railing as I dared.

Below the meniscus of the water in the glass bottle of the dispenser, a swath of forest was reflected in miniature, upside down.

I took one step too many and the bird darted away.

With nothing to lose now, I leaned on the railing and breathed in the best air I'd tasted since coming to America.

'Good morning.'

I turned around. Kristen, wearing knee-length frayed jeans, a strappy red velvet top, and old sandals. She closed the door to their bedroom behind her.

'Hubby still asleep?'

'Mm,' she nodded. 'Dead to the world.'

She came forward and leaned on the railing too.

'I was watching a hummingbird a moment ago.'

She squinted out into the fresh day. I studied her freckles, began to count them.

'I was up at dawn,' she replied, 'and I saw deer feeding down there in the clearing.' She nodded towards a plastic contraption on a pole about thirty yards from the house. 'A doe and her babies.'

Feeling as if I'd been bested in some nature epiphany contest, I was tempted to make some snide Bambi comment, but held back. Today I wanted to be nothing less than charming. And that desire had nothing to do with my softly-softly mission. I didn't know what I was going to do. Or should I say, I didn't know how far I was prepared to go. I didn't know if I could hold back any longer.

I said, 'If this is the real Texas, I think I want to emigrate here after all. It's heavenly.'

'Well, another Irishman got here before you.'

Before I could think of a suitable reply, she turned around and said, 'And it's high time he woke up.'

'See you downstairs at breakfast, Kristen.'

She went back into her bedroom.

I should have teased her. That's what a Mountain would have done. Charm is daring.

Even the light in Eleanor's spruce kitchen had a freshly scrubbed quality.

I was not the first person down to breakfast.

The people from Houston, two jolly, ample couples, were already tucking into freshly squeezed juices, warm bread, thick coffee, and a type of omelet dense with diced meat and vegetables. The dish,

130

I learned, was called migas. Eleanor was busy making more at the stove.

I sat down and the hyper-friendly Houston people introduced themselves. Mike and Sharon, Rex and Tina. Ordinary folk, polished by affluence.

When I said I was from Ireland they reacted as if I'd announced I'd come down from a passing comet. I didn't ruin the effect by telling them I was a lawyer.

Then Kristen appeared, looking bleary-eyed and brittle. At the table she was polite but distracted, making limited eye contact, even with me. Especially with me, perhaps.

The Houston people were unconcerned, probably assuming she was not a morning person. But all those mornings in Maverick that's exactly what she had been. She had been as bright and positive as the new sun.

What had happened in the last five minutes? What was wrong?

Obviously John Paul was wrong, or something was wrong with John Paul. I hadn't heard any fighting through the rough wall that divided Ghost Dance from Half-Moon, but that didn't prove anything. Perhaps John Paul had a silencer for arguments too.

And now enter Mr Wrong himself, in rare form.

'Hello, folks.' He extended a big hand as he strode across the bare floor. 'I'm JP and I'll be your breakfast partner this morning.'

The Houston people laughed – Kristen didn't even smile – and the men actually stood up (heavily, grabbing their napkins as they tumbled off their laps). As John Paul shook each of their hands in turn, and then finally mine, he reminded me of his father, and his father's golden handshake in a long-ago household.

Kristen was in a much better mood by the time she drove us into Winter's Mill. Especially when we passed a sign on the windy way welcoming us to the 'Town of Antiques'.

I asked, 'How much of that name is hype?'

John Paul replied, 'Winter's Mill brought itself back from the dead with this strategy.' He looked at me archly. 'Sometimes you have no choice other than to reinvent yourself. It's a survival strategy.'

But the conversation was essentially about things, not people, and John Paul seemed to be content to keep it that way.

Winter's Mill was really a village, or as close to the idea of a village as I had yet seen in Texas. Three streets intersected at a broad circle, in the middle of which was a quaint stone well. Whether it was the restored, authentic navel of the town or a faux feature lately installed I couldn't tell.

Kristen, the trained eye, said that most of the Victorian houses had been built in the last five years. They certainly looked authentic, with their Corinthian pillars, carved eaves, and fish-scale slates.

We parked by the ornate marbly courthouse – its entablature studded with inlaid blue stars – and walked along the very Western elevated arcade of the main street. The town centre was comprised of nothing but antique shops and restaurants that called themselves cafés.

The morning got hot and the village got busy. I was glad of the shady arcade. Assistants carted mahogany-framed mirrors and chests-of-drawers across the main street. We browsed and wandered and rummaged and poked.

After less than an hour John Paul said that he'd meet us in one of the café-restaurants. He was bored, he announced bluntly, and wanted to amuse himself by reading the fifties pulp fiction novel he'd picked up for a few dollars in one of the junkier places. Its dog-eared cover featured a black revolver, a red sports car careening over a cliff, and a terrified platinum blonde with conical breasts.

'We'll join you for lunch,' Kristen said, speaking for both of us. Dust motes swirled in the tension between them.

When he'd walked out through the saloon swing-doors of the

cavernous establishment we were currently in, I said, 'At least he can't drink here.'

She continued to study the delicate wooden toy in her hand, but did smile.

Later, in another, even larger store, she said:

'What I'm really looking for is the kind of turn-of-the-century bureau, with lots of wonderful little drawers, that I saw up here the last time. For my study at home. I'm kicking myself for allowing John Paul to convince me that it was too much of a hassle to bring it back to Maverick. I mean, what is a sports utility vehicle for if you can't use it to transport wonderful furniture?'

'I couldn't agree with you more.'

With that out of her system, she lightened up. 'Well, that's what I'm officially looking for, but of course, I could easily be seduced by something else.'

She picked up one of a pair of iron objects that looked like elongated jumping jacks.

'What are they?' I asked.

'Knife rests. I need them.'

She got them.

And indeed Kristen had to return to the Blazer several times with the smaller trophies she picked up, the smaller finds she made searching for her late Victorian bureau. The battered lampshade she picked up for a few dollars looked worthy only of the rubbish heap.

'Where are you going to put that?' I asked, fondly sceptical.

'In the guest room,' she replied seriously, 'after I've découpaged it with some Chinese paper.'

And that was Kristen, I thought. She could see the possibilities of something, or someone, damaged.

I said, 'I'm sure the next guest will appreciate it.'

She shrugged, picking up another knick-knack and scrutinising it.

'I'm not sure there will be another guest.'

A slit of a smile after she said that, as if she'd discovered a hidden detail in the curio she was turning in her hand.

I took it as an encouragement.

Meanwhile, with a lot of solicitous advice and encouragement from Kristen, I was scouring the town of antiques for the perfect gift for my fiancée. Something very Suzette. That was, after all, my official motivation for being in Winter's Mill. But I found it hard to keep my mind or my imagination focused on Suzette – on her tastes, her partialities, her desires. Instead, I kept on thinking about buying something for Kristen, something perfect for her. Secretly, I was looking for that bureau too.

Eventually, with my stomach complaining about hunger, my sinuses complaining about dust, and my eyes complaining about the endless dense junk, the possessions, detritus, and photographs of the obscure dead, I'd had enough, and settled on a porcelain jar, mint condition, circa 1895, fired and hand-painted locally with the craft and care of the old country.

She would love it. At two hundred dollars, it was one of the most expensive small items in that particular store. I didn't haggle, as Kristen hinted I should. In fact, I would have paid more. I didn't just want to buy a gift. I wanted to spend money on my distant fiancée.

I signed the American Express receipt with relief, then turned to Kristen.

'Well, that's Suzette taken care of. Shall we join John Paul?'

Suzette would never receive that ambivalent gift.

That lunch was the only meal besides breakfast that I had with John Paul where he did not (could not) order a drink. And what a difference a little enforced spin on the wagon made. Take alcohol out of the equation and John Paul Mountain became quite a reasonable fellow.

I couldn't help but think of his mother's sobriety that night in the rue des Saltimbanques.

After avocado and bacon sandwiches, the house specialty at the Rocking Horse Café, we went back to a deserted Lightfoot Inn to pick up our swimming things. Kristen and John Paul wanted to bring me to a place called the Green Hole.

'One of our special places,' John Paul told me, as we waited for Kristen to finish changing.

I nodded agreeably, dampening down a sudden flare of jealousy.

We rolled and meandered through the bright hills for a good twenty minutes. Then John Paul pointed out a primitive sign and turned down a flinty road. It went through a dark wood for a few hundred yards before arriving at a wooden entrance booth.

After a brief wrangle, John Paul allowed me to pay for three daily memberships. He drove down a sloping, grassy field of mobile homes and parked the Blazer in a shady lot of brown earth. Even before we got out of the Blazer we could hear the pleasing shrieks of children.

The Green Hole was true to its name. Limey water pooled deeply in the bend of a river. John Paul informed me it was called the Ponderosa. Overhung by huge cedars, only the very middle of the hole sparkled under a sky so blue that it had hints of space-black. At the shallow edges of the hole were pale rocks large and flat as kitchen tables.

One particularly thick cedar, which jutted right out over the natural pool, almost to the centre of it, had wooden steps nailed into its flaky trunk. Eight or ten tanned children and teenagers were queuing along the muddy river bank, waiting for their turn to clamber up the steps, grab the black iron ring tied to the end of an old rope hanging from the longest limb, swing out over the glinting green depths of the pool – and let go.

We set up camp under another cedar, this one set back from the river. Kristen spread a large blue blanket on the brown earth. John Paul stripped off his clothes, revealing loud red Bermuda swimming trunks. He charged into the water, yelling for the cold. He could have been mistaken for a large child. After swimming far out into the pool, he turned and beckoned us to come in.

Kristen shook her head, half embarrassed, half indulgent. She slunk out of her aesthetically faded jeans and red top. Underneath she was wearing a dainty purple bathing suit, with ruffled folds above her bijou breasts.

'Coming in?' she said.

'Yes, certainly,' I replied, grabbing a tight shoe.

Not waiting for me, she tiptoed to the green water's edge.

I felt rather self-conscious being reduced to my skimpy, thigh-tight, grey Irish togs, which could so easily be mistaken here for underwear: every other male in sight, young or old, was wearing the same knee-length baggy trunks as John Paul – swimwear both brash and modest. I needed the camouflage of that thick water.

Now, I'd swum in cold water before – try the Irish Sea on an October morning – but that green chill was really a shock. After so many days of Texas heat I couldn't believe that Texas water could be that frigid.

I swam out over the stone tables, out past my depth, out to where Kristen and John Paul were, dodging children lolling in large black rubber tubes.

No sooner has I reached them than John Paul dived under the water, almost to the bottom of the pool, with its carpet of green swaying fronds, and swam breaststroke – those long Mountain arms describing a generous half-circle – all the way back to the stone shallows.

'How does he hold his breath that long?' I asked Kristen.

Treading water beside me, she replied, 'I've been holding my breath for two years – how about that for a trick?'

It's hard to shrug when you're chin-deep in water.

John Paul scrambled out, dripping profusely, and joined the queue for the swinging tree. Remembering that night he'd dived into the pool at Logan Hollow, I was expecting an expert turn – perfect execution.

His wife turned her back and began to swim out steadily, barely disturbing the green water, moving silently towards the river proper.

I watched her over my shoulder until it hurt, then turned back to see what John Paul was up to. He had advanced, impatiently, to the base of the tree. A bony-limbed boy, perhaps seven or eight, was tentatively scaling the crude rungs to a point where he could grab the ring, still swinging from the teenager before him who had bombed into the water. The child finally teased the rope into his hands and, with surprising abandon, swooped out over the water, letting go with exact perpendicularity, dropping cleanly into the water, re-emerging with a brief, clean shriek. He was, of course, a veteran.

John Paul was ready to go, his feet straddling the upper, wonky rungs, one hand on the tree trunk, the other stretched out over the rippling green water, waiting.

It happened very quickly.

He got hold of the rope, slid his hand down to capture the ring, grabbed it with the other, and swung off the tree, his body elongating in such a way that it briefly reminded me of the figure we'd known in Dublin.

The way he swung across the water would have done Tarzan proud – except he failed to let go of the rope, either as he swung out or swung back. Whether he hung onto the ring because he'd missed his chance to drop into the safe deep water or, as it struck my eye, whether he most determinedly swung all the way back to the pool's edge, I don't know.

All that's certain is that John Paul crashed into the scaly trunk, slammed into it with the side of his body. If he was letting go of the ring to soften the blow with his arms – if he tried to save himself at all – I didn't catch it, I didn't see.

He certainly let go when he bounced back off the rugged trunk, falling, knees bent, into the smooth-rock shallows.

A man and a lanky teenaged boy bolted into the water to help him, confirming that this was serious.

By the time Kristen and I reached dry ground – she swam so ruthlessly fast that she overtook me – John Paul's rescuers had carried him to a patch of soft grass, where he sat with a small white towel over a scraped and bloody shin – and a dazed smile on his face. The right side of his body was broadly bruised.

Before asking her husband if he was all right, Kristen thanked the people who had helped him out and supported him, even offering to replace the bloody towel.

So I said to him, 'Will you live?'

Still smiling, John Paul replied, 'Not without a real drink.'

I helped him up; he dropped the towel.

Kristen continued to thank our fellow swimmers, laughing nervously, beginning to chatter.

Because I was bolstering a limping man, she caught up with us before we reached our spot.

John Paul looked down at his skinned shin.

'I'm still bleeding,' he said with detached curiosity.

'So bleed awhile,' I heard Kristen mutter as she bent down for one of their own towels.

So why had she swum so surprisingly fast to shore?

John Paul laughed jaggedly.

I eased him down onto the warm fuzzy blanket. Kristen plonked herself down beside him, put on her shades and looked back over to the daredevil's cedar. That veteran child was making another perfect swing.

By the time shadows started to grow out fast from the high cedars, John Paul was back on his feet again, still limping a little but restless. He went back in the water, pleased by the need to wash off his scraped leg, even swinging off the black ring again, his old fluency restored. I should have taken that opportunity to have a serious, responsible conversation with Kristen about that little self-destructive episode we had witnessed, but I deliberately missed it. I didn't want to draw any more attention to John Paul. I wanted to draw attention to Peter Dagg, when the time was right.

Kristen lay prone on her tartan blanket, one brown knee raised, eyes resolutely closed behind her turtle-pattern shades. Still, I felt sure she could sense me noting and cross-referencing the snubby nipples showing through her bathing suit – that she knew what John Paul was up to, that she knew what I was up to. All the same, I looked.

I could have sat beside her till nightfall, but after he'd dried off, John Paul was restless again.

'Shall we hit the road then, guys?'

Kristen raised her shades and squinted open one eye.

'Why the rush?'

John Paul shook his head innocently. 'No rush. Though I am hungry.'

'Where do you want to eat?'

'How about the place we found on the road to Kerrville?'

Both eyes now.

'The place with the membership, you mean?'

John Paul shrugged, pursing his lips and then allowing a smile through.

'That's the one.' He nodded in my direction. 'I think Pete would like it.'

Kristen raised herself up on her elbows.

'The view or the overpriced beer?'

Another boyish shrug. 'They go well together.'

So we went to this restaurant – Bill Bob's Bistro – in the middle of nowhere, watched the sun go down behind the rough hills, sitting out on the crazy-paving terrace which, by the time we left, was almost full. Last time they had been up here, John Paul complained, it had been almost empty. Their special places, it seemed, were being discovered, one by one. I wondered if soon they would all be entirely overrun.

I ordered a bowl of Provençal stew, for old time's sake. Her son didn't seem to recognise the dish. In any case, it wasn't as good as Nessa's. But then again, how could it have been?

In fact, John Paul drank far more than he ate – that membership, which only he took out, allowed him to order five-dollar beers for an initial fifteen-dollar investment. And he worked hard to make that investment pay.

Kristen hardly ate at all, and it wasn't because she was too busy talking.

As good as the food was, as good as the location, I was relieved when John Paul paid the bill – I didn't even pretend to dispute this one with him: I did not want this to be my treat – and we started back to the Lightfoot Inn.

Perhaps there I could steal some time alone with his wife.

It was solid night by the time we arrived. On the front porch we met the people from Houston on their way out. They were delighted to see us, delighted to see John Paul.

'And where are you guys off to?' he said.

If you didn't know he was very drunk you might well have thought he was just being very friendly.

They were off to Bum's.

'That's where we were last night,' John Paul pointedly informed them. 'A fine establishment, a fine establishment.'

It was Rex who asked the question that John Paul had primed:

'Well then, why don't y'all come back there again with us tonight?'

John Paul turned to Kristen and me, appealing, his eyes bulging with drink and mischief.

Kristen wouldn't look at him directly. She shook her head, her features stern in the porchlight.

'No, you go – go with Peter.'

'Why won't you go with me?'

I could see that the Houston quartet were getting a little uneasy. I was sure they were beginning to regret bumping into us.

Now Kristen looked her husband in the eye, even gave him a steely smile.

'Someone has to be in good shape to drive back to Maverick tomorrow,' she said.

John Paul took this well, nodding and protruding his lower lip, a model of tipsy reasonableness.

Then he looked at me, almost vulnerable in his need for company, the company of one of his old tribe. In any other circumstance I would have gone with him; Mountains need people like me. And what a good opportunity, I reminded myself, to advance the cause of my mission. I had spent very little time lately alone with John Paul.

But these were no ordinary circumstances. I saw a window of opportunity here, a different kind of opportunity, and I now discovered that I was intent on going through it, if I could.

With a weak, apologetic smile, I shook my head softly, ruthlessly.

I felt as if I were studying myself, learning more about myself every moment. So this is the kind of man I was – this is what I was capable of. I was surprised, but not in any immediate way guilty.

John Paul's mouth tightened. I was sure he was going to forget about the whole thing, go storming in through the screen door. If he was on the point of doing so, Rex saved the day, saved the night. He came up behind John Paul and slammed his hand down on his shoulder blade. (The *violence* of friendship in this land.)

He said, 'Never mind your friends wimping out on you, buddy, you can ride in the Explorer with us.' He winked at Kristen. 'Don't worry, miss, we'll take care of him.'

A giddy thought: did Rex somehow assume that Kristen and I were the couple, and that John Paul was our friend – that he was the gooseberry of our threesome?

The Houston foursome began to move towards their vehicle.

Kristen and John Paul were staring at each other, edgily, although I suspected that there was more going on between those locked eyes than I could pick up on. (I felt like a substitute warming up on the sideline, itchy to get into the game and replace the star player, now burnt-out.)

Words Rex threw over his shoulder broke their connection. 'C'mon if you're coming, bud.'

John Paul was coming. He gave both of us a little mock-bow and said, 'I'll be back before I'm missed. Behave yourselves.' When he turned to go, I wanted to slap him on the other shoulder.

We watched the red tail-lights of the Explorer disappear and reappear, then disappear for good on the winding road. What now? I turned to Kristen, put a diplomat's smile on my face. She had her slim arms crossed and looked cold, though the night was thrumming with heat.

'I'm going to make some mint tea in the kitchen,' she said.

I nodded, non-committally. Did she mean tea for two? Was this an invitation?

While I was still thinking, cautiously, about my next move, she went inside, the screen door closing with a *clat* behind her.

I sat down in one of the big solid rocking chairs and stared out at the lower range of stars until I felt a dignified amount of time had gone by. I did not want Kristen to think I was following her. I did not want to think that I was following Kristen.

Sauntering rather self-consciously into the kitchen, I was irritated to see that she was not alone – Eleanor was sitting across from her at the round table. They weren't drinking tea but wine, a beaded bottle of white between them. The women looked very comfortable in each other's company already, and I wondered how welcome I was, despite Kristen's history of signals, or the series of signs I had taken as signals.

As I stood there I was also standing in the kitchen of the Cloud House, getting ready to loosen my tie.

The invitation came. 'Won't you join us for a glass of wine?' Eleanor said formally.

Kristen, looking over her shoulder at me, added, 'Proprietor's special reserve.'

'Well, in that case . . .' I replied, and sat down beside my friend's wife.

The wine was excellent, and so was the company. It turned out that I was quite wrong. Eleanor wasn't a problem, she was a catalyst. We all loosened up, especially Eleanor herself. After refilling our glasses she began to tell her story, the story of how she came to be the lady of Lightfoot Inn.

She was not a native Texan. Born in Baltimore, educated at Boston College, she had lived with her husband in Fort Lauderdale for nearly fifteen years, running her own real-estate business.

'So what brought you here?' I asked.

She smiled. 'Treatment.'

South-west Presbyterian in Maverick happened to be the most advanced hospital in the world for her rare form of cancer. She said the words 'my oncologist' as if she were trying to keep a firm grip on them. Once she became an outpatient she rented an apartment in the University District rather than make the twice-weekly trip from Florida. Her marriage broke up. She started taking classes in Native American Studies, a long-delayed passion. In remission she discovered the Hill Country. Five years ago she had bought this property and had been working on it, and her master's degree thesis on herbal healing, ever since.

'Any regrets?' Kristen asked.

Eleanor nodded. 'Yes. That I didn't leave Fort Lauderdale a decade ago.'

It was good to hear her story. It was even better when she gracefully excused herself, told us to help ourselves to tea and home-made shortbread, and left Kristen and me alone together. I was glad we'd both had a few glasses of wine.

'Interesting woman,' I said, to say something.

Kristen's response was an edifying non sequitur. She leaned her cheek against my shoulder and put her arm around my back. The thrill of the physical.

'Oh, Peter,' she said, in a sad, sisterly way.

I looked down at the beginnings of those pearly breasts. The Caution Horse was about to die. I was arranging a perfect execution. Putting my arm around her stiff back, I stroked her smooth arm, once.

'I think I'll sit out on our balcony for a while,' I said, and broke away gently.

Kristen brushed a wisp of straw-hair back behind her ear.

'I'll clear away the glasses,' she said, looking at the table. 'And then I'll join you.'

Charged, I walked through the house quickly, taking the stairs two at a time, and taking a deep breath when I stepped out onto the upper porch. What would be the most nonchalant position to be found in? Rocking in one of the big chairs? No, that might look a little arthritic. Instead, I selected a wooden pillar to lean against and stared up and out impatiently at the stars. The moon was full, crisp. The set-up was too good to be true.

After a slow five minutes – my right arm was becoming numb from leaning so long – Kristen appeared at the double doorway. She had taken off the thin cardigan she had worn downstairs, leaving that red top.

As she moved closer – sauntering, with a pursed smile – I saw how the Hill Country sun had darkened her small shoulders. I stood up straight.

'Dear Peter,' she said, and hugged me, resting her head against my chest. 'Dear dear Peter.'

'Dear Kristen,' I replied lightly.

'You don't know how great it's been to have you here this past week.'

I tried irony. 'Oh, I can imagine.'

'No,' she replied, her voice catching. 'You don't understand. This is the closest thing I've had to a normal life, a normal happy life, in a long, long time.'

I felt a warm spot on my shirt, and realised that Kristen was crying.

Softly I said, 'New Plantation, the dealership, weekend getaways – all that seems normal enough.'

Despite her tears, I relished holding her. No: understatement. The tears made it even better.

She exhaled sharply, scornfully. 'Life with John Paul Mountain can never be normal. Not any time, not any place.'

If I had been a true source of consolation, of counsel, I would have said at this point, But you still love him, right?

But I did not say that. I did not say anything, and it felt good. For too long I had been a verbal creature. I had grown clever, and stagnant – middle aged at twenty-seven. I stroked her hair, and that felt even better. This trip to Maverick, I saw now, was not about the Mountains, it was about me. It was my liberation. The Mountains could go to hell.

Kristen sighed softly. I sensed my moment, and I took it. I brushed the soft underside of her chin, causing her to look up at me. Her eyes were glistening blue. She smiled, heightening the effect, and I kissed her lightly on the cheek, then lightly on the lips. I closed my eyes and moved in with an unambiguously sexual kiss.

She responded, energetically, and we went into a tight embrace.

My legs weakened and my erection strengthened. At first I was worried that she would notice it, creeping up her thigh, and then was past caring.

On the kissing front I got very intense, making my first tongue incursion. She broke away and I thought I had blown it. But she was smiling, and stroked my cheek.

'Not so *fast*.'

So we began again, not so fast. This time I paid more attention to her cues – I felt they were cues – slowly increasing the pace from the demur to the dirty. At the same time, I told myself that it was time to move this business inside; I had received the first hint of moistness from the waistband of my briefs. (Some men have a problem with premature ejaculation; I suffer, occasionally, from – what should I call it? – immature ejaculation.)

By now Kristen had French-kissed me back – albeit for a token reciprocal visit – and back in her mouth our tongues were whirligigging around each other. I readied my hand to grasp her right breast, trusting I'd encounter stiff nipple.

Suddenly she broke away, putting her hands up in avowal.

'No,' she said, not with anger but with resolve. 'I can't do this. I can't do any more. She'll notice the difference.'

Bewildered, I replied, 'What do you mean she'll notice the difference?'

'Suzette – who else?'

'I know who you're talking about, Kristen.' I had to check the anger in my voice. 'What makes you think that I'll be going back to her after – this?'

She threw her eyes up violently.

'Oh for God's sake, Peter, don't be ridiculous.'

'What do you mean?'

Oh I knew the answer, knew the answer to that.

Kristen was shaking her head. 'I don't know what you expected. This – *that* was nothing.'

'Nothing?' I stared at her, discovering the depths of my anger – towards her, towards myself.

She withered a little, shaking her head more contritely now.

'I'm sorry – sorry if anything I've done or said in the past week led you to believe that I was ready to do anything ... significant, with you. Don't you understand, Peter?' She laughed, all too convincingly. 'You think this is the first time I've flirted as a married woman? I've had other moments like this – I'm sure you have too—'

'As a matter of fact, *no*.'

She didn't pay my interruption much heed. 'And it doesn't mean that I'm ready to do anything ... irreversible. I'm still committed to my marriage, believe it or not.'

'Oh, I believe it – now.'

She frowned. 'And what about you?'

'What about me?'

'What about Suzette?'

'Leave Suzette out of this.'

She laughed and shook her head. 'And you're calling me a hypocrite.'

I turned a sharp eye on her. 'I never called you a hypocrite. You've just got a bad memory.'

'And yours is even worse.'

Now, that hit home. Wasn't constructing a shining career based on my superior memory?

'Nobody's ever accused me of that before,' I murmured.

'So then you haven't forgotten.'

I humoured her.

'What haven't I forgotten, Kristen?'

'That you have your Mountain, and I have mine.'

And with that she turned on her heel and went back inside. A few moments later their bedroom light came on.

Our balcony scene was over.

*   *   *

Later, much later, after a tortured walk under the starry starry sky, I lay on the left side of my roomy bed, and listened to the return of John Paul Mountain. Windows open, I heard the Explorer crunching up the gravel road, and the hoopla when the doors opened: twangy banter, a female shriek, and a Dublin accent. I swore I heard a rough, randy Dublin accent down there, as if Jerry Mountain and not his son had come back from Bum's.

That house of wood was like a radar: I could track John Paul's path with all too vivid precision: screen door, stairs, bedroom. He woke Kristen up with his shameless coming in, or more likely Kristen was awake still, waiting for him. The last thing I wanted to hear was their muffled conversation, but since I couldn't block it out, it vexed me how close I was to making out the words . . . especially with my ear against the wall.

And when they raised their voices I convinced myself that I was making sense of what they were saying. An argument was slowly building, with a lot of whimpering and recrimination. Over John Paul's drinking, for a start. And then of course the drinking was just a symptom of the chronic disease that was their marriage. The terminal disease that was the Mountains.

As the argument increased in intensity and volume, I swore I heard her call him a bastard and him call her a slut. Now they were positively shouting. I began to worry that the people from Houston, preparing for bed below all this, would call on Eleanor to intervene.

Suddenly something hit the wall with a shudder, dislodging my ear. Other knocking sounds followed on hard. They were throwing things, they were throwing each other. John Paul was getting violent. Forget Eleanor – surely I had to intervene myself, break them up.

Then the fight seemed to find its locus, its essential battleground. Squeaking sounds, rocking sounds – they were battling on the bed.

The pace increased – the struggle was getting more desperate. Who knew what John Paul was capable of? This assault had to be stopped. I clambered down off my bed and went to the door.

Then I heard Kristen shriek, and shriek again, and took my hand off the door knob. The shrieking went on for a depressingly long time, each shriek outdoing the last, until I was sure nobody in the Hill Country, let alone Eleanor in her separate quarters, was asleep. At last John Paul, provider of orgasm-on-demand, moaned. (I was moaning quietly to myself, resisting the temptation to bang my head against our mutual wall.) The fight was over. Both parties had scored a big victory.

I did not cut off my ear. Instead, I sent that dreamcatcher – a furry frisbee – sailing across the room.

In the morning, I emerged from Half-Moon late. The Houston people were gone. Eleanor was sitting with the Maverick couple at the round table. Did I see her smile into her coffee mug after she said good morning? John Paul and Kristen were sitting across from each other, both polishing off, to judge from the smears and traces on their earthen plates, a hearty fry-up. Eleanor got up to make mine.

'Just some scrambled egg for me,' I told her.

'Sleep well?' John Paul asked, his mouth not quite free of a large chunk of sausage.

'Quite well,' I said, testing my grapefruit juice.

Kristen didn't ask me anything, just sliced a last piece of bacon with a petite smile on her face. Was she masking her embarrassment or her contempt? In any case, I hated her right then, at that homespun table. Hated them both.

I said, 'What time do you think we'll make it back to Maverick by?'

John Paul looked shocked. 'You're so eager to get back? I thought you liked it better up here.'

Now Kristen wasn't smiling. She stared at her husband across the table.

'John Paul.'

John Paul looked at me still. 'You don't want to tour the brewery in Hamburg?'

'John *Paul*.'

I shook my head and gripped my mug. 'Another time, perhaps.' I sipped the coffee. It tasted gritty this morning. 'I really need to phone my friends in San Francisco to let them know when to expect me. And I left my little black book in New Plantation.'

John Paul smiled. 'How unlike you, Peter.'

Kristen said, 'Whatever Peter needs to do he needs to do.'

'Oh, of course. I just hope he won't leave until Tuesday.'

This was an allusion to the arrangement we had made before leaving Maverick. Helen was organising a little farewell dinner in my honour for Monday night. I had thought that by then I would have done as much with John Paul as could be done, my way. Of course, before this watershed weekend I hadn't understood what my way really was, and where it would lead. Yes indeed, I needed to say farewell.

I said, 'I wouldn't dream of leaving without saying goodbye properly to Helen and Bob. They've been so kind.' I smiled for the first time that day. 'You've all been so kind.'

The drive back to Maverick took half the time, and was twice as long. I sat in the back on my own, and still felt oppressed by the empty friendliness all three of us exuded. Barbs, taunts, and recriminations would have been better than the pap that passed for conversation as we sped south. But as the land flattened and the development thickened, surest signs that Maverick lay ahead, the silences between the small talk stretched.

Kristen, driving, turned on the radio, hit a button pre-set to

Variety 101, a saccharine mix of adult-friendly top forty hits and old reliables from the seventies and eighties. I had all but tuned it out when, as we hit the Beltway, the one country song I could stand came on: the one held tenuously together by a Theory of Evolution metaphor (with Creationist undertones), the one saved by the yodelling, throaty trio of female voices. I had heard the song at least six times, travelling around with John Paul, but never like this. Gone was the Nashville instrumentation: not a banjo to be heard, not a slide guitar in sight. Synthesisers filled the vacuum. A jittery, insistent rhythm track had been added, plus a smattering of techno squeaks and squawks.

I hated it – the remix, I mean. It was . . . a travesty. Nowhere near country enough for me. I took comfort in those Southern, sassy harmonies.

Back at New Plantation the Mexican fog was gone but the air still had an acrid taste; it tickled the back of my throat. It was a relief to get inside and, once inside, a relief to get upstairs. I told my hosts that I had calls to make, and that was true, but the calls I made were not to Garrett and Katy in San Francisco; they were to Suzette Mountain in Dublin. I wasn't exactly sure what I was going to say to her but I knew I needed to talk.

But Suzette didn't answer, not the first, second, or third time I tried her mobile. Instead her recorded voice picked up each time after the sixth purr; I didn't even know she had a recording, so umbilical was Suzette's connection to her mobile.

I didn't leave a message, not knowing what my message was. Puzzled and irritated, I even phoned her home number, but all I got there was an answering machine featuring one of Suzette's media mews-mates.

Though I gave up on Suzette, for now, I was in no hurry to rejoin John Paul and Kristen downstairs. Instead I stretched out on my ample bed and considered my position. Status report: my mission had failed. I had failed. So why then was I beginning to feel so rawly free?

It would take a long, slow drive across America to answer that question. Suddenly the prospect of leaving Maverick – and heading further west – thrilled me. It was time to re-establish contact with Garrett and Katy.

When the phone rang, I didn't pay it much attention. I was too busy calculating American distances and Korean speeds. In any case, it was picked up downstairs after just a few bleats. But the daydream I was having of a small yellow craft sailing through a painted desert was abruptly dissolved by a triple knock on my door.

I got off the bed feeling panicky, as if I'd been disturbed mid-masturbation. Shyly I opened the door. Kristen. With a tease in her voice she said, 'It's for you, Peter.'

Part Three

DUBLIN, TX

Between closing the door – softly-softly – and putting the portable to my ear, I wondered how on earth Suzette had got hold of the correct number . . . then too easily imagined her phoning the wrong number and charming some anonymous Maverickian into serving as directory inquiries.

'Suzette,' I calmly predicted.

I heard another extension click off: John Paul had been listening.

'Hello, sweetie.'

How to handle this? I decided to go sentimental. 'It's funny, but you sound so close.'

'It's funny but I am.'

'What do you mean?'

'I'm in Atlanta.'

'Atlanta, Georgia?'

'That's the one.'

'What are you doing in Atlanta, Georgia?'

'We're about to get on a train.'

'Who's *we*?'

'Jerry and I.'

'Jesus Christ, what are you and your father doing in Atlanta about to get on a train, Suzette?'

'That's as far as the train from New York goes.'

'What were you doing in New York?'

'We were meant to get a connecting flight yesterday at JFK but Jerry couldn't take anymore flying after the flight over. Things

155

got a little turbulent over the Atlantic. The poor man was very heroic, Peter, in his own way. But he insisted on taking ground transportation to Maverick.'

'Why in God's name are you coming to Maverick?'

'I would have thought, Peter, that you couldn't wait to see me.'

'I can't – but I was envisaging an emotional reunion at Dublin airport.'

'Well, this can be emotional too. I know that John Paul probably won't want to be there, but I'm sure Kristen can drive you.'

'Where?'

'To the Maverick train station.'

'Are you sure there is one?'

'Peter, sweetie, why else would they have issued us a ticket?'

'Absolutely. Of course you're right.'

'Three o'clock tomorrow, OK?'

'Three o'clock?'

'Sorry it can't be sooner.'

'Oh, that's OK.'

'Promise you'll be there?'

'Darling, hope you don't mind me asking this but why are you doing this to me?'

'We're just coming to lend you a helping hand, sweetie. Seems like this task is proving a little bit much for you. Jerry and I talked it over once you told me you were going to that Hill Country. Will you be there?'

'Of course I'll be there,' I snapped back, and thumbed the connection button.

If I have a philosophy of lying it is this: get it over with. In their white cavern of a living room, I handed Kristen back the phone with a well-moulded smile.

John Paul, sprawling on the couch, said, 'So how's my little sis?'

'Just fine.'

Kristen asked, 'How's Dublin?'

'Cold.'

Leaning in a corner was the pole they used to change the fat, recessed light bulbs at least twenty feet above our heads. With its splayed head, it looked like a particularly cruel kind of medieval lance.

I said, 'Listen, since it's my last day tomorrow, I thought I'd try to take in a few more Maverick sights. Not that I expect either of you to take another day off work to show me around. I thought if I had a guidebook or something that would give me a few ideas . . .'

John Paul said, 'Yes, we do unfortunately have our work to do.'

Kristen said, 'I have exactly what you're looking for, Peter.'

She fetched it from her study, and I spent as much time as possible that evening studying the book alone in my bedroom. *The Scoop on . . . Maverick*, from the Scoop Cities series, was a tall, glossy paperback with a shot of a high-noon Consort Tower – this was the good old days – on the cover.

Inside was a Maverick I did not recognise: a cosmopolitan yet affable city of intimate restaurants and sidewalk cafés. It had a frequent bus service which conveyed the eager citizenry to a plethora of artistic spectacles. Nature refuges were plentiful; master-planned communities did not exist. Neither, apparently, did train stations, until I spotted a small map buried deep in the third appendix. Tomorrow I would be driving the Haiku to a grey dot on Arkansas, a long street in the shadow of downtown.

Next I turned to the thick section on accommodation, swiftly deciding to consider only those hotels in the luxury bracket, the places with the symbol $$$$ beside them. I was ready to inflict whatever damage on my credit card, and my sanity, it took to get Jerry and Suzette in and out of Maverick with the minimum of fuss.

Listening carefully for any extension pick-up – there was none – I phoned and booked a suite at the downtown Tranquillity Bay. It sounded like a good place to talk some sense into a father and daughter who had gone beyond the pale.

If I had my way, Dublin would come to Maverick, and Dublin would leave again, and John Paul Mountain would be none the wiser.

I almost missed it, initially registering the crummy structures on my right as the shell and forecourt of a run-down petrol station. Then the Haiku's suspension took a pummelling and I realised I'd hit railway tracks. I did a crunchy U-turn and crept back over them. Those cars weren't filling up, they were parked. I rolled up beside them on the chalky ground and got out. I didn't lock my door – I couldn't believe anybody would want to steal the Haiku, even in this ruined neighbourhood. A glance through one of the windows of the cinder-block main building revealed a rudimentary ticket counter and a set of purgatorial wooden benches that I assumed was the waiting area, though the few faces I could see suggested more a state of detention.

Running parallel to the one-way, rusty tracks, the platform consisted of a rectangular slab of concrete, ineffectively sheltered by a slim grey canopy. Underneath it there were people alert enough to be counted as waiting. In fact, one man, an elderly black gentleman wearing a tiny trilby hat, was looking with some intensity up the tracks, craning his neck. I craned my neck too, and saw nothing but the pastel downtown skyline. But the old man kept it up, and sure enough after several minutes, as if he'd drawn the locomotive our way magnetically, a yellow light, like a rising minor sun, appeared on the horizon. It was five minutes to three. I decided the man was an authority.

'Excuse me, is this the train from Atlanta coming in?'

He turned to look at me, take me in. 'Ain't no other one.'

I nodded. The engine grew taller, its headlight shimmering.

The man in the trilby turned to me again. 'That's my daughter on that train.'

'Excellent.'

'Who are you waitin' for, son?'

'Oh, relations. Loved ones, I suppose.'

Mirth on the old man's face. 'You suppose?'

I shook my head. 'No, no. Definitely loved ones.'

The train arrived with such shrill deafening force that, for a wishful moment, I wasn't sure it was going to stop at all, the driver perhaps unwilling to dignify this raw spot with the status of station. But stop it did, and from half a dozen doors passengers trickled out.

I saw Suzette almost straight away, wearing a skinny blue dress, but instead of looking around for me, she turned back to the open door to receive one, three, five items of luggage from a tall stooping figure, who then straightened himself and scanned his new surroundings before stepping down from the train with the gravitas of a man who thinks he's being filmed.

My eyes met Suzette's and she made a beeline for me, long Mountain arms outstretched. She embraced me as if I were a trapeze she'd almost missed, but the kiss was better, the kiss had spirit and the tease of sex in it. I didn't deserve it, of course. Remembering my experiences with Kristen, I tried to make my response as enthusiastic and amateurish as it had always been before.

'You made it,' I said.

'*You* made it,' she replied.

'Just about.'

Jerry approached us as if he were walking on a red carpet and porters had attended to the bags stacked on the concrete. His suit was immaculate but his handshake was a limp imitation of what it once had been. Trying to keep my smile this side of respectful, I said, 'Welcome to Maverick, Mr Mountain.'

He surveyed his surroundings, mouth rumpling. 'Are you sure this isn't Mogadishu?'

'It gets better, Jerry.'

Suzette was looking around too, looking for people. 'Is *she* here?'

'No, no,' I replied apologetically. 'I thought it best to come and meet you alone. I'll explain. We have some talking to do, you know.'

'We do indeed,' said Jerry.

'But how are we going to get out of here?' Suzette wanted to know.

'I have a form of transportation.'

Suzette and I struggled with the luggage over the rugged ground; Jerry travelled light.

'Is this a taxi?' Suzette asked, dropping two suitcases beside my yellow peril.

'Do you see a taxi driver, sweets?' I replied.

'It'll do grand,' Jerry pronounced. 'Safer than that bloody plane, that's for sure.'

He actually helped me load up the luggage. Another struggle. If there had been four of us we'd have had to leave one suitcase behind.

Jerry then opened the front passenger door and managed to pull the seat-back forward. He waved invitingly. 'Come on, Suzette, let's get out of this humidity. It smells like the Devil farted on this place.'

I didn't think it wise to try to explain to Jerry that Maverick wasn't normally this bad.

A rare moment followed – the sight of Suzette no longer standing her ground. She got in the back, with a suitcase for company, which allowed Jerry to sit up front, as he'd wanted. Weighed down, the Haiku rolled across the car park as if it were a bed of nails.

Back on Arkansas, heading towards downtown, Suzette said, 'Would you mind turning up the air-conditioning, please, sweetie.'

'That's as high as it goes, I'm afraid.'

'Where did you rent this piece of rubbish, Peter?'

A mechanical laugh. 'Actually, I didn't rent it. I own it.'

'You bought a car to pick us up from the train station? Sweetie, you do care.'

'Well, no. It was a kind of gift.'

'A kind of gift from whom?'

'Mr Wingate. Bob.'

'Well, you must have made quite an impression. Must have been hard for him to part with it.'

Jerry was staring ahead at the looming downtown skyline. 'Now that is a magnificent sight. If only we had something like that in Dublin, but of course the shower who are in charge now don't have the imagina—'

'I'm glad you like it,' I interrupted, 'because that's where you two are going to be staying. Tranquillity Bay is a four-star hotel.'

Jerry's bitter expression turned into a puzzled pout. 'But John Paul doesn't live in the downtown.'

I beat time on the Haiku's bony steering wheel. 'You actually expected that John Paul and Kristen would have the guest bedroom all ready for you?'

'See, Jerry, I told you,' was Suzette's clipped commentary from the back. Her father ignored her.

'Well, we know that room's yours, Peter,' he said reasonably. 'If their house is full up – though I doubt it – we're quite prepared to stay with Kristen's parents. From all counts they should have enough space to squeeze us in.'

Exasperation felt good. I allowed myself another fix. 'But Jerry, what makes you think John Paul would be OK with that? He's very possessive about the Wingates.'

Jerry shrugged innocently. 'I assumed that you would have . . .

smoothed things out.' He looked over at me pedantically. 'We did give you advance warning.'

My mouth opened once more, but this time no words came out. There was too much to say, too much to protest. After twenty years of dysfunction, betrayal, and substance abuse, Jerry Mountain expected me to have smoothed things out overnight. I was summoning up a grunt of contempt when Suzette put me on the defensive.

'Sweetie, you have told John Paul we're coming, haven't you?'

Luckily at that moment I became involved in tricky negotiations for entry onto Washington Parkway. But once that was accomplished I had to give some kind of answer. 'Not exactly,' I said.

'That means no,' Suzette replied.

'Yes.'

Jerry veiled his face with one of his nimble hands. 'Oh Peter, Peter,' he groaned. 'Why did we bother to send you out here in the first place?'

His lamentation suggested that he had personally funded the mission at great expense. As for his question, I had no answer. I wanted to know the answer too.

'But you have told *her*,' Suzette said.

'No.'

'Her parents?' she asked with a kind of shy desperation.

'Not yet.'

Suzette exploded. 'Oh sweet Jesus, Peter Dagg, Jerry's right – why the feck did you agree to come here if all you were going to do was sabotage us? Don't you realise this is our family you're playing with?'

Dazed, I could only reply, 'It's a four-star hotel. It has spectacular glass elevators.'

'Lifts, Peter,' Suzette snapped back. 'The word is lifts. You're beginning to speak American.'

'Lifts, elevators – it doesn't matter,' Jerry said loftily. 'I, for one, am not staying in any hotel in a city where a child of mine is living – and in some splendour, from what I hear.'

'Make that two vacating the room,' Suzette added.

'But it's booked,' I protested.

'*Un*book it,' Suzette said.

'Where will you sleep?' I asked.

'On the streets if we have to,' Jerry replied. 'God knows it's warm enough.'

I knew that was bluster, classic Mountain bluster, but I resolved to be as mature as I could in handling the situation. Somebody had to be.

I said, 'So you don't want to go to the hotel – OK. Where do you suggest we go?'

'To see John Paul,' Jerry replied, his tone suggesting that I'd presented him with an elementary mathematical problem.

'But what if,' I replied as delicately as I could, 'what if John Paul is not quite ready to see you?'

This too was easy – addition, subtraction. Suzette answered, 'Then we go see the Wingates. They seem like nice, reasonable people.' Was she implying that I, her fiancé, was not a nice, reasonable person? 'After all, they did invite us to the wedding. I'd like to reciprocate, in person.'

'So let's go there,' Jerry suggested amiably, as if we were deciding the destination of a Sunday outing.

With an epic sigh, I did a deliberately dramatic U-turn which provoked curt expressions of terror from both Suzette and her father. Fleetingly, I was at peace.

'Do you know how to get there from here?' Jerry asked with keen suspicion.

'Not exactly,' I breezily admitted. 'But it wouldn't hurt for us to do a little tour of Maverick. It's a fine city.'

And I meant it.

*   *   *

Once I rediscovered the Splendora freeway, things got better, for Suzette and Jerry at least. They expressed no more doubts about my sense of direction. Jerry couldn't get over the parade of commerce along the feeder roads. 'Spoiled for choice, spoiled for choice,' he said, approvingly. 'Peter, you'll have to help me book one of these places. I think the four of us, and Kristen of course, should go out for a bite to eat one of these nights. And you're the Maverick expert.'

I gripped the steering wheel so hard I was afraid it would snap. I wasn't sure what made me angrier: the wilful mythmaking that he and John Paul would be reconciled so easily, or the nerve he had to start his favourite Dublin game here: hinting that dinner was going to be his treat, then actively ignoring the bill when it arrived. Why he felt it necessary to play it with us, of all people, I don't know. Pride, perhaps.

'There's the man we're going to see,' I said, pointing to a Suburban Bob billboard as I prepared to parachute the Haiku off the freeway.

'Looks like a very reasonable man,' Jerry said. 'The kind of man you would buy a used son off.' He chortled to himself.

'Looks sexy,' Suzette noted.

Logan Hollow shut them up, as I thought that nonchalant display of affluence might.

Only when we passed a gleaming white Logan Hollow Police car did the Mountains find their voices again.

'That's what we need in D4,' Jerry laughed. 'Our very own police force.'

'Gardaí for the glitterati, you mean,' Suzette deadpanned from the back.

I wanted to add a point of information: technically, Jerry didn't live in Dublin 4 any more. But, as usual, I decided it was wiser to keep facts to myself.

*   *   *

The Wingates' sprinklers were on, but they were not home yet.

'Probably at the dealership still,' I said, getting back in the Haiku.

'And John Paul?' Jerry asked jumpily.

I nodded. 'He'll be there too.'

'Well, let's go then.'

I started to shake my head, revving up for an absolute refusal to go that far – it was bad enough I'd transported this time-bomb to the Wingates' home; to bring it to their business, their baby, would be too much. To my surprise, Suzette leaned forward, put a tempering hand on her father's shoulder, and spoke for me:

'No, Jerry, let's wait here. We've come far enough.'

He opened his mouth to argue, then seemed to absorb what she'd said; he raised his eyebrows and shrugged. At that moment, he suddenly looked old and out of his depth. I even felt sorry for him.

'Well, can't we just drive around or something until they get back,' he said finally. 'I think it's better to be late. Through two decades of public life, that's always been my policy.'

I stopped feeling sorry for him. He was behaving as if he'd discovered the Wingates were throwing a surprise party for him and he was too polite to let on he was in the know.

'No, Jerry,' I replied. 'I agree with Suzette. Best to wait here.'

I didn't want to meet that police car again. Kristen had told me how the Hollow cops pulled over cars they didn't like the look of on the slightest pretext. They wouldn't have to look at my Haiku for very long.

Jerry said, 'In that case let's go sit by that pool of theirs I've heard so much about.' He put his hand on the crude door handle.

'No!' Suzette and I ordered in unison.

Jerry looked exasperated. 'Ah, sure you're no fun at all, you pair.'

Just then a flash of brilliant red metal caught my eye and I looked across the lush front lawn to see a vintage convertible pulling into the driveway. Helen Wingate was home. The Corvette slid behind us going towards the triple-door garage at the side of the house.

'Stay there,' I told father and daughter.

They stayed there. I walked around the corner and met Helen walking towards me. She was wearing shiny workout clothes.

'Peter, honey,' she said. 'I didn't expect you so soon. I've just picked up the food from Yummy's. But since you're here maybe you can help me take everything inside.'

I put my hands out as if I were trying to encourage her to stop shouting in a library.

'Helen, Helen, something's happened. I've got some people with me.'

'Some friends? Oh that's fine, honey, you should see the hors d'oeuvres plate I got. Bob will be eating the leftovers for a week.'

'No, I mean some people from Ireland.'

'From Ireland – but Peter, honey, that's wonderful. You know how Bob and I feel about people from Ireland.'

'Well, actually, it's not just any old people from Ireland.' I paused, and not for effect. 'Helen, John Paul's sister and father are here.'

She stared up at me, her full, rose-painted lips parting slowly. Then her face became animatedly warm again – the usual Helen. I looked behind me, where she was looking. There they were. I stood aside. Helen was shielding her heart.

'Well, this is just a magical surprise. How wonderful to meet you.'

She stepped forward to greet Jerry, who had his hands waiting for hers.

'Jerry Mountain,' he said, his voice as mellifluous as it had been on television years ago. 'And I have to say that the thrill is all ours, isn't it, Suzette?'

His daughter was by his side.

'Yes,' she said, with a courteous smile. 'It certainly is.' She shook Helen's hands with a little more restraint. 'We've heard so much about you.'

Helen turned to me with a look that tried to make me complicit in her joy, then once more took in her guests from heaven.

'Just wait till Kristen gets here.'

I had to say it. Somebody had to say it. 'Just wait till John Paul gets here.'

The way the three of them didn't look at me just then, you'd swear that I'd just ruined an innocent moment with an obscenity.

We sat in the Pentagon. Helen was the perfect hostess – cocktails, bowls of cashew nuts, healthy servings of tact. Jerry clearly felt right at home, as if the sprawling house were some fine country residence he was staying at ex officio, his Chequers, his Camp David. Suzette, sitting beside me on a deep couch, was more restrained – pensive, in fact. I squeezed her hand from time to time. She squeezed back, infrequently.

A huge truck the colour of champagne turned into the Wingates' driveway. Helen put down her daiquiri. 'Bob's here,' she said teasingly, as if he might be bringing home the necessary savvy to defuse this situation. She slipped away.

'Mr Discount,' I said archly, the way I'd been taught to in the Law Library. Anything to break the tension. My tension.

'Now, Peter,' Jerry replied in a grandfatherly way, 'don't be condescending. These people are obviously a very nice class of Americans.'

Suzette breathed in acidically, bowed her head, and began to rub her brow with her long fingers. She snapped out of her frustration when we heard Suburban Bob's approach.

'No! . . . No! . . . No!' he growl-shouted as he came through the house. He filled the entrance from the hallway, standing on the marble with his thick Prussian arms outstretched in quiz-show host amazement.

'Well, how the hell are you people!'

The people got to their feet. Jerry came forward and did his head of state thing. Bob looked genuinely enchanted as he shook the foreign dignitary's hand over and over again. 'So this is where John Paul gets it from,' he kept on saying. 'This is where John Paul *gets* it from.'

Then he turned to Suzette. I have to confess that he turned on the charm so deftly, so sweetly that I almost swooned. I had seen Suzette Mountain look many things during the course of our relationship but I had never seen her look bashful.

Then Bob turned to me.

'And here's the guy responsible for it all,' he said heartily. If he'd slapped me any harder on the shoulder at that moment I might have been ejected from the room.

I'm sure this little idyll would have continued for several more minutes – Helen came back, adding grace notes to the proceedings – if it hadn't been for the sobering sight of two more vehicles coming down Pecan Circle. The Camero, followed by the Blazer, both of them going too fast for this tranquil street, as if a chase were in progress.

Suzette looked at me, hard, deep; and I in turn studied her so long that I thought I saw bruises around her eyes. I can't explain this in so many words – this is not a court case – but I knew then exactly why she had come, and just how badly I had let her down.

This time Helen did not leave the room to soften the surprise. For once both Wingates and Mountains did nothing, said nothing. They just stood there, waiting for Hurricane John Paul to hit the room. Jerry had this smug look on his face, as if he were one of those crazy old men who are convinced their beachhouse is strong enough to withstand the storm surge. I had this last-minute desperate notion that I should run through the pool room and warn him, tell him to get back in his Blazer and flee. But I did nothing. Or perhaps I did something by not moving from Suzette's side.

We heard them coming in through the back door, talking cheerfully enough, heard the smack of the Wingates' Fort Knox of a fridge opening, and John Paul saying, 'I'm telling you it's the Gilsons, they were dying to meet Dagg.'

So he had seen us as he sped by the Pentagon; seen us and failed to recognise his family. I wished to goodness he had.

We saw Kristen coming through the pool room, wearing a smart skirt and white blouse, shades planted high on her pinned-back hair. She slowed as she took in the delicate tableau prepared for her. Stopping on the threshold of the Pentagon, she tilted her head back slightly and, as if she had cut herself, breathed in sharply through her lower teeth.

Then John Paul appeared at the entrance from the hall. The shock didn't register on his face, but the long blue glass in his right hand tilted; water spilled on the marble; a lump of ice shattered.

'Ah!' said Jerry, taking a bold step forward. 'Here's the man himself!'

His son shook his head. 'No.'

Jerry stopped. His son continued, 'You're not here. You're *not* here.'

Suzette spoke up. 'John Paul – sweetie – we're here for you.'

I noticed his wife had now come into the room.

John Paul shook his head again, appearing to wrestle with his tongue. Finally he said, 'Then I'm not here.'

He spun around on the wet marble. We heard him slam down the glass on the Wingates' antique hall table.

'John Paul!' his father said, his tone suggesting disapproval at the way a six-year-old is coping with a vol-au-vent. He looked around at all of us for counsel. 'Where is he going?'

Looking through the pool room, I caught a glimpse of him marching through the kitchen towards the back door. Jerry barged past the Wingates yelling his son's name. I stopped him. 'I'll go after him, Jerry.'

'He's my son.'

'It's my job.'

I looked over at Suzette, expecting, I suppose, some loving, tearful smile of endorsement for that admission, but all I got was a very constricted nod. I couldn't blame her for that.

'All right,' her father said with a harrumph. 'But let go of my arm.'

'My pleasure.'

'Go, son,' Bob said.

I nodded and went. But I'd only got as far as the pool table when the Blazer roared down the driveway. I toddled back into the Pentagon.

'Well, with all due respect to the pre-owned division of Wingate Chevrolet, I don't think I'm going to catch him in my car.'

Helen said that of course Jerry and Suzette must stay with them, for as long as they needed to be in Maverick. Bob concurred, but not with his trademark exuberance. We were sitting at their dining table, eating my farewell. There was more than enough to go around – the usual Maverick cornucopia, this one featuring prawns the size of my fist. Even if John Paul had stayed, there would have been more than enough. Besides, Kristen hadn't eaten more than a few bites of the plainest available pasta. She kept leaving the table to use the phone, and kept returning a minute later in brittle silence. We knew that the only contact she was making was with her own answering machine.

The third time she came back to the table her mother reached across and stroked the downy top of her hand. 'He's going to be fine, honey. Just give him time.'

'How much time does he need?' Kristen snapped back.

'That's what we've been wondering,' Suzette told her.

'That's always John Paul's solution,' Jerry added, from the end of the table. 'Run off, run away. Well, off with him – that's what I say.'

I looked away from him with simmering disgust. Bob refreshed himself with some Chianti, holding his wine glass as if it were a tankard of ale. Then he spoke. 'That's a fine boy you have there, Mr Mountain, sir, all the same.' He raised his glass, a Viking toast.

Jerry had opened his mouth to speak before Bob had quite finished – how parched his tongue looked, despite all the white zinfandel he had been drinking – but then the toast got to him, and for a moment I was sure that he was going to cry. He didn't, thank God, but it was a close call.

Although you could hardly have called the atmosphere festive, it did get better after that. The eye of the storm, I can see now. The spine of the conversation was between the two proud fathers, the sole highlight of which came when Jerry tried to explain the rules of hurling and Gaelic football using analogies from other sports as disparate as ice hockey and Graeco-Roman wrestling. All this from a man who had once proposed that the Irish language be banned as a means of modernising the country more rapidly.

Then the phone rang all around that vast house, a whole chorus of extensions. Kristen sprang out of her seat and almost ran into the 1981 wing. A door closed, the phones fell silent. Twice we heard shouting, Suzette and I looking at each other pensively both times. When Kristen came back into the dining room, looking proud and tense, I was sure she had some major news to announce: John Paul was at the airport, John Paul was threatening to jump from the sixty-fifth floor of the Gastec Tower. Instead she looked at me – stared at me, more like – and said, 'Peter, it's you he wants to talk to.'

At that moment I felt as if Bob and Helen Wingate were the only people in the room who didn't hate me. Was it my fault if I was the only one John Paul wanted to confide in? Yes, it probably was.

I put my barely soiled napkin down and stood up. The open door in the 1981 wing, I discovered, led into Kristen's old room. I tried not to take in much about the room's decor – it made me feel a little perverse to be in here, among the frills and the fripperies of her girlhood – but I couldn't help noticing her passion for collecting antique dolls (some of whom, in their Victorian silks, could have been painted by Singer Sargent himself) and her penchant for anything to do with fish.

I picked up the purple receiver as gingerly as a loaded gun.

'This is Peter.'

'Where are you?'

I could tell from the light sonic haze he was on a mobile. Beside the phone was a purple pen and a block of notepaper bordered with her name in turquoise letters: Kristen Kristen Kristen.

'I'm in one of the guest bedrooms,' I replied.

'No one there with you?'

'Oh no.'

'Good. And that's the way I want it to be when I meet you, Peter. You're the only one I trust now, do you understand?'

'I understand, John Paul. Don't worry, I'll come alone.'

'Bob will try to follow you.'

'I dare say he will. But then again, I can be persuasive.'

He laughed. 'Oh, very persuasive. Listen, how soon can we meet?'

'How soon do you need to meet?'

'Now.'

'Now?' I sighed. 'OK, I'll try to get away as soon as I can.'

'Get away.'

'I will, trust me. How about somewhere quiet where we can sit down and talk, like that Persian place we went last week?'

'No, not there.'

'The Thai place?'

'No, not a restaurant, Peter. Listen, I'm breaking up. Can you find a pen and paper?'

I had not heard much interference at all. 'Hang on a moment,' I said, staring at the purple pen and the Kristen paper, 'I'll look.' I counted to six and added, 'Found them.'

'Take down these directions.'

When I finally put down the phone, I not only tore off the map I'd improvised from John Paul's instructions but also several other pages, so that no trace of where I was going would be left behind.

In Maverick I learned to regret my smartest moves.

The others had abandoned the abundant table. I stepped into the Pentagon wearing a poker face. Bob was on his feet. Everyone else was sitting on the comfortable furniture uncomfortably, except Jerry, who looked far too comfortable. And he was the first to speak:

'Well, what does the ungrateful little shit have to say for himself?'

'Jerry,' Suzette hissed through her teeth.

Her father spread his hands eucharistically and answered, with the voice of reason, 'We came all this way, I went through a take-off and a landing for that fella—'

'I'm sure John Paul will come round to appreciating all you've done for him.' This firm intervention from Helen seemed to pacify Jerry, for the moment.

Bob got back to business. 'Where is he?'

'Driving,' I replied.

'What did he *say*?' asked Kristen, staring at me.

I stared back. 'He said he wanted to meet me, at a restaurant.'

'Which restaurant?'

I smiled my regret. 'I'm sorry, Kristen, but I promised your husband I wouldn't say. Right now he needs to talk to me, alone.'

She didn't acknowledge this; instead, she turned to her mother and said, 'I bet it's that McCourt's.'

Helen winced, then nodded.

Her husband held up a meaty hand. 'Listen, folks, if we let Peter here have a little one-on-one time with JP, it can only do some good. All we can do is stand by and make assists.'

I took this to be an endorsement. 'Thank you, Bob. And I'm sure you agree that there's no point in anyone following me at this stage.'

I caught Kristen and Suzette trading dissatisfied expressions. Tacit bonds were developing between the sisters-in-law.

Bob stared at me with aggressive sincerity. 'Absolutely.' The half-moons below his eyes were waning nicely. 'We can't afford any fielding errors now.'

Jerry Mountain nodded sagely, as if he had been about to say the exact same thing himself.

If I had not spend those interlude days getting lost in but also finding my way around Maverick, I don't think I would have had the confidence to have gone so far, alone, to meet John Paul. The directions he'd dictated were true and the few wrong turns I took were my own fault and not fatal.

I headed through Logan Hollow, driving away from the certain corridor of the Splendora freeway. As instructed, I got onto Castleberry, one of the city's infinite streets. It took me north for almost a hundred blocks, a numb landscape of apartment blocks, shopping centres, churches that looked like shopping centres and, increasingly, strips of grassy nothing. At last, I found Sawdust, turned right, located the power sub-station that passed for a local landmark, and made a U-turn to get onto Parchment – the street we were to meet on.

Though he had told me I would see the Yellow Hog Tavern on the left, I cautiously scanned both sides of the road. The Haiku was happy cruising along at twenty-five. Everything was bright, everything was bleak. After a dozen blocks – just as John Paul had estimated – I saw it, on the left, a low red-brick structure with a corrugated iron roof, more bunker than building. And there was the Blazer, looking far too new for this non-neighbourhood. Apart from his SUV, the small sandy parking lot was deserted.

I parked close to him, feeling uneasy when I turned off the ignition and the automatic seat belt released me. When I got out, I thought it safer to leave the Haiku unlocked, ready for a quick getaway, or whatever kind of getaway my Maverick car was capable of. I put the thin key in one trouser pocket and Kristen's slim mobile in the other.

Cautiously I walked around to the front of the bunker-bar. The neon signs in the windows were dead. Putting my face to the glass, all I could see were chairs upturned in darkness, a fat dead cockroach, and spent peanut shells. Then I heard my name being shouted and I turned around to see John Paul across the street, business shirt loose over sagging khakis, beckoning me. He was standing by the gate of a chainlink fence half camouflaged with creepers. And behind the fence was an encampment of . . . ice cream vans. He beckoned again, called my name again.

My lawyer self told me to get out of there, get back in the unlocked Haiku. But I ignored that voice, and crossed the hot road. After all, I had never been drawn to the Mountains for reasons of safety.

He smiled when I reached his weedy side of the street.

'Glad you could make it.'

Looking through the fence, I could see that the two dozen or so ice cream vans were battered and rusty, their CAUTION CHILDREN signs cracked, the swathes of lollipop stickers on their sides bleached and peeling. They were parked in haphazard rows, on concrete where grass and weeds were breaking through and oil lay in puddles. I could not tell whether this was an ice cream van parking lot or a graveyard.

'What is this place, John Paul?'

'Well, it's not a master-planned community, is it?'

'You knew that bar was closed, didn't you?'

He replied with a boyish smile and shrug.

'So why are we here?'

John Paul sighed. 'Let's just say I didn't want to alarm you by asking you to meet me in such an . . . unconventional location. But since you're here, Pete, c'mon. I have something to show you.'

What did I imagine was really going on? Well, I had some notion that this lot was John Paul's territory and that stashed, perhaps, in one of those abandoned ice cream vans was a wealth of pure white powder. Yes, I was expecting the revelation of some shadow-life – this was John Paul Mountain – some operation that would make daft, perfect sense.

I followed him through the open gate.

Not a word passed between us as we weaved between vans, one junkier than the last, several leaning decrepitly to one side where a bald tyre had gone flat. John Paul reached the back doors of a van with a particularly high roof, its CAUTION sign black on orange. A single square sticker advertising a thick ice cream sandwich caught my eye, so I didn't see him draw the gun from under his shirt as he turned around. It was stomach-sinkingly familiar – the Sauer Parabellum .357 he had shown off that first evening in New Plantation. Was this then the last day of my vacation? I realised that even if there had been anyone passing by the lot – and as I forlornly heard my mother say, there had not been a sinner around when I crossed that road – John Paul had brought me to a spot where we could not be seen. A spot for perfect execution.

Even though I was immediately and profoundly afraid, I was also genuinely irritated, and that's what I expressed:

'John Paul, what are you playing at?'

'I'm not playing at anything, Peter,' he replied with great control. 'Question is, what have *you* been playing at these last ten days?'

Cautiously, I raised a reasonable hand.

'Please, John Paul, you've made your point. Joke over.'

He smiled. 'But, Peter, I've hardly begun to make my point. Now, answer the question.'

I sighed: a tremor came out. This situation was far too real, far too American for my liking. I managed to say:

'Well, of course, of course I came out here with the intention of convincing you to come back – for the wedding, my wedding.'

He shook his head, like an indulgent school teacher, and raised his gun.

'That's not what I'm talking about. That's already been established.'

'So what are you talking about?'

As soon as the words were out I realised I'd been too bold. I held up contrite, shielding hands; the muzzle of the Sauer came close to touching my fingertips as John Paul jabbed it forward. Now I understood that this cold rage was no put-on. This was no – simple – joke.

Honesty was not the best policy now. Honesty was the only policy.

'Do you mean Kristen?' I asked humbly.

He raised his eyebrows in mock-surprise. Or perhaps I was just wishing it was mock-surprise.

'Ah, yes, Kristen, my *wife*. Yes, tell me about my wife and you.'

'Nothing happened, John Paul. Trust me.'

'Nothing happened in the Hill Country?'

Another tremulous sigh. 'You know nothing happened in the Hill Country.'

'How do I know?'

Even with my life on the line, I found it very hard to break through my fastidiousness. 'You do because . . . you two clearly got on like a house on fire that last night.'

A chip of a smile. 'No thanks to you.'

But I realised in that tight moment something I could not say: it probably was thanks to me that they'd reconnected with such abandon at the Lightfoot Inn. (I hadn't heard any screams on any night at New Plantation.) Not only had I been their guest, I had also been a player in their game.

I was the devil, and I was the dupe.

Gravely I replied, 'I'm sorry if I haven't been a very good friend, John Paul. I can understand why you're angry.'

Those last words were my biggest mistake. As red-faced as he was in the sticky heat, a white glow spread from his eyes. There, in that moment, I knew what it felt like to believe you are about to lose your life. How does it feel? Exactly like that – a heavy, thick loss.

'But you don't understand why I'm angry, Peter.'

No, I didn't understand. What could be worse than messing around with his wife – at the very least intending to make him a cuckold – yet another humiliation that the old John Paul Mountain would probably never even have conceived of having to face? What could be worse? He enlightened me:

'You really stepped over the line when you brought *them* here.'

So that was the worst betrayal of all – messing around with his family. Did he consider it a kind of incest? I feared he did.

I replied to the charge slowly, deliberately, 'But you must believe me – I did not bring them here.'

'Give me one good reason why I should believe you.'

I couldn't. Instead I said, 'They came of their own accord, John Paul! Come on, is it like me, your Caution Horse, to pull a stunt like that?'

If I had heard this argument myself, I would not have been convinced.

Sickeningly, John Paul smiled. 'After that little stunt in the Hill Country, I wouldn't put anything past you.' He sighed. 'Do you know what you are, Peter Dagg?'

After a numb silence I asked, 'What am I?'

'You are the worst creep of them all.'

Though I bristled with the injustice of what he said, some

part of me – my heart? – heard only a confirmation of what it secretly feared.

I said quietly, 'Whatever you say, John Paul.'

In reply he clicked something significant on the side of the gun – the safety catch, I could only presume.

'Do you know what I've wanted for a long time, Peter?'

'What?'

'To die.'

For a moment I couldn't quite believe my ears. 'Really?' I replied, putting too much croaky hope into the word.

He nodded. 'But instead I've decided that today somebody should die for me. They can take care of me at a later date.'

The baking chamber at the dealership appeared in my mind. I heard Suburban Bob's brag: perfect execution. And I saw John Paul's finger curl around the trigger. My mouth fell open:

'Remember my e-mail?'

He winced with puzzlement, irritation, but the gun dipped a little.

'What?'

'The e-mail I sent you when you – very kindly – invited me to stay.'

He threw his eyes to the burning heavens and trained the gun again, as if I'd distracted him from finishing some chore. I blurted:

'Nessa – I had something to tell you about your mother, the last time I saw her.'

He lowered the gun and stared at me sourly. 'Yes, I remember. I didn't imagine you could tell me anything I didn't already know. You may be my shadow, Dagg, but it's still my family.'

I stared back and said, 'Why take your anger out on me?'

That question cheered him up. He palmed the gun and with a sweep of that hand pointed out the sad vans. 'Because I have you here.'

'But only miles from here there's someone whom you should really be angry with.'

I was amusing him greatly. 'Jerry? How could that man cause any more outrage?'

Thankfully, I had a good answer to that question. Serious as a World Service newsreader, I said, 'At the time your mother died your father was actively planning to have her killed.'

For all I knew, I might have been telling the truth.

John Paul did not react, though a sheen of sweat formed on his brown forehead. He blinked and said, 'And how would he possibly be able to do that?'

I raised my eyebrows frankly, looking at him as intently as I dared. 'You think he surrendered all of those offshore accounts?'

Again the non-reaction, and then the sweaty blink. 'Why would he do it?'

I opened my mouth to speak – this was all coming too easily – then hesitated. Oh, motivation. I couldn't do without it, but to offer it could put me in more peril than ever. But when I saw his fingers slipping into position around the ready Parabellum again, I forced myself to speak:

'Because he found out that she'd cheated on him – cheated on him before he'd ever had a chance to cheat on—'

'Bullshit,' John Paul snapped, but through his eyes I could see that something inside was cracking.

I began to edge away, wondering if I could make it behind the next van, a battered blue vehicle, before he could react, accurately.

And when he pointed the gun at my forehead I ordered myself to run, and froze. I felt myself plunging inside, like lead.

'Move,' he said.

'What?'

'Move, I said,' and John Paul indicated with the Sauer that I should start walking back the way we came. This time he followed. I ghost-walked to the gateway. When he came alongside me, the gun was nowhere to be seen. Looking up and down the road, he said, matter-of-factly, 'You'll give me the keys to your car, I won't give you the keys to my ute.'

'Understood,' I replied.

We crossed the road, John Paul now walking impatiently ahead of me, revealing the gun-lump under his shirt-tail. Back outside the Yellow Hog Tavern, standing next to the big vehicle that I couldn't use, I hazily noted that John Paul turned and gave me a patronising blink when he turned on the ignition, and that when the seat belt wrapped itself around him, he reached up to the clip above his shoulder and undid it. Even if I had been thinking clearly at that moment, I don't think I would have read any more into that gesture than a desire not to be so confined in a confining space. John Paul – the ute man – did look ridiculous in that Haiku.

After he had gone, speeding off down Parchment as if he'd utilised a secret fuel injection system in the Haiku, I coughed through the dust left in the wake of John Paul's sudden reversal, felt nauseous and faint for the best part of a minute, and then remembered the mobile I had not surrendered. He should have made me turn out my pockets.

As I waited to be rescued, I had time – too much time – to make sense of what had just transpired. Under Irish law merely pointing a gun at an innocent party constituted a serious offence, and I couldn't imagine that even in Texas what John Paul had done was without criminal implications. Then again, I did not feel like an innocent party, and in my brief phone conversation with Bob Wingate I hadn't mentioned any gun. I would have to, I now realised. Other lives were now in danger – though the prospect of John Paul shooting his father did have a certain poetic appeal.

I paced up and down the crunchy parking lot, trying to ignore the useless SUV. Why he had stolen the Haiku I had no idea. I put it down as yet another reckless Mountain eccentricity. What I was much more concerned about was that last accusation he had made – that I was his shadow. It was a sting to the soul. I could see my whole past reconfiguring around that charge. The volatile gun in my face was nothing by comparison.

I was in shock, of course.

'Good to see you, Bob.'

'Hop in, Coach.'

He waited until I'd got my seat belt on, then stormed back through the vast banality that lay between the scene of my near-death experience and cosy Logan Hollow. In the Silverado I felt insulated from the nothingness of the neighbourhood, grimly optimistic that clout and sanity – Bob Wingate's brand – might get us out of this mess.

'Let's keep a sharp eye out for that yellow car,' Bob said, not without humour. 'I've got a feeling your friend is going to stick closer to home than you might think.'

'Bob, my friend is armed.'

He absorbed this with equanimity but the humorous lilt in his voice now disappeared. So, even by local standards, the situation was serious. 'Well,' he said, 'no blood, no foul. But all the same, I'll call Travis Holbien.'

Without taking his eyes off the road, he punched in a number on the speaker phone in front of his cup-holder.

'Who's Travis Holbien, Bob?'

'Cop we know.'

I wanted to say more, ask more, but there was an answer on the second ring.

'Yellow?' said the speaker phone. For a moment I thought this was some telepathic anticipation of the colour of the car we were looking for, before realising it was a deeply Texan form of address.

'Travis, Bob Wingate.'

'What's happening, Sub!' the cop replied exuberantly.

'Got a situation, Coach.'

'Shoot.'

'Emotionally disturbed son-in-law driving around town with a gun. And not driving a Chevy. Advise.'

'D'you reckon he has a licence for that gun?'

'Can't confirm.'

'I don't believe he does,' I said.

'Who's that with you, Bob?'

'Fine young Irish lawyer by the name of Peter Dagg. He came over to help.'

I trusted Bob wasn't experimenting with irony.

'From Ireland too, huh? Tell you what I'm going to do, Bob. I'll call in an APB to dispatch straight way. I'll drop by and see y'all at Pecan Circle on my way into work. Now, you wouldn't happen to have that plate number, would you?'

'We can swing by the dealership and pull it up on the computer.'

'No need,' I said. 'I memorised it the day I drove it off the lot.'

Bob looked over at me reverently. 'Well, looks like we have a pinch hitter.'

I had no idea what that meant; I was flattered.

'What makes you say that, Mr Dagg?'

Maverick Police Department Officer Travis Holbien had detective-level eyes. Their blue irises had egg-white haloes which only accentuated their truth-seeking stare. What was this trim man, who seemed to have swatted away early middle age, still doing in uniform? Wasn't any friend of Bob Wingate a team captain?

We were standing around one of the minor islands in the Wingates' expansive kitchen. Everyone who had a stake in John Paul Mountain was there. The mood ranged from Bob's oceanic calm to Kristen's imploding distress; this was obviously a level beyond the recklessness he'd displayed before in his short marriage. This was not just another lost weekend.

Officer Holbien had dropped by on his way to a shift downtown, where, according to Bob, he was a stalwart in the organised crime task force. He was currently staring at me. I had just, cautiously, advanced the theory that this was no ordinary case of weapons possession.

He pressed me. 'What makes you think he may do some harm?'

'Well,' I said, tapping my foot on the pastry-coloured tiles. I felt as if I was being cross-examined by Maurice Swarbrigg. And I had seen grown men and politicians cry when Maurice had cornered and dismembered their equivocation. Officer Holbien didn't have Maurice's despicable eloquence, but Maurice didn't have Holbien's X-ray eyes. The best ploy, as it was with Maurice, was to be unstinting with the truth.

'The thing is,' I said matter-of-factly, 'I think John Paul is out to murder his father.'

'That's a scurrilous *lie*,' Jerry spluttered, brandishing a brittle finger across the island's chopping-board surface. 'If we were in a different jurisdiction I'd sue you for slander.'

Without quite looking at her father, Suzette put a moderating hand on his shoulder. She looked as if she were doing some private grieving already.

'Go on,' Officer Holbien instructed.

'You're not the only one, Jerry,' I said encouragingly. 'Suzette may also be in danger.'

I saw Kristen wince. Did she feel marginalised by John Paul's wrath?

'And Kristen too,' I rounded off.

Helen clutched her daughter. I wasn't sure who was leaning on who for support.

'Anything else?' Holbien asked, sounding a little impatient.

I nodded intensely, remembering John Paul's flirtations with self-destruction. 'I think . . . he might turn the gun on himself,' I said, finding the phrase ready-made in my CNN memory.

Tears massed in Jerry Mountain's eyes. Suddenly I saw him as nothing more than a sad old man standing over a smashed family. I saw him as nothing more than a father.

'But on the other hand,' I added quite truthfully, 'he may do nothing at all. He might just be upset.'

Travis Holbien obviously didn't think much of that theory. He looked at Bob. 'You have a gun in the house?'

'Sure,' Bob replied.

'Keep it handy.' He turned around. 'And I think the rest of y'all should go to a hotel.' The tense non-reaction to this idea was a measure of its popularity; I chose not to mention that I already had a reservation at a very secure hotel. 'Just for t'night,' Holbien continued, 'or until we can find John Paul and talk him down from this. The most important thing is that nobody gets hurt. Simply not a good idea to cluster together in such an obvious location. Just in case.'

His tone implied that if we didn't take his professional advice there was little he could do.

'Have you phoned the Hollow Police?' he asked Bob.

He nodded. 'A few minutes before you arrived. They said they'd drop by.'

'I'm gonna go by there right now. I'll arrange for an officer to stay around, low-key, until we can sort this out. Situation warrants it now.'

''Preciate it, Travis. You're a starter.'

'Any time, Sub.'

Helen showed him out.

'Let's sit down and think about this,' Bob said, his authoritative survey of the other concerned parties making it more than a suggestion. We went into the Pentagon. Bob and Helen remained standing.

'If only this were happening in Dublin,' Jerry lamented. 'Then at least the gun part of the equation wouldn't be there.'

'Don't be too sure,' Suzette replied.

'We can't go to some hotel,' Kristen cut in, briefly throttling the air for emphasis. 'I want to be out there looking for him.'

'You heard what Officer Holbien said,' her mother warned. 'That could be dangerous. . . . What if you do find him? He could do some harm.'

'I'll take that chance. I know John Paul.' She seemed to deflate. 'Peter is right. He's mostly a danger to himself.'

'But, honey,' her mother said. 'It'll be like trying to find a toothpick in a haystack.'

'I know his haunts, Mom. Some of them, at least.'

'I'm all for it,' Jerry pronounced.

'Me too,' Suzette added in a level voice.

We were, I realised, all looking at Bob Wingate. The ends of his moustache were turned down in a meditative frown. He nodded weightily. 'We should look for him. Once the cop from the Hollow Police gets here, the home base is covered. I want to get some of the boys from the dealership on this too. In fact, I'm gonna call Steve Dildine right away.'

'Do you think that's, uh, absolutely necessary?' I asked, feeling a little like the boy who cried wolf. The way Bob and Jerry stared at me I soon felt embarrassed by my question.

I held up a peacekeeping hand. 'Whatever we need to do,' I said.

Suburban Bob did what needed to be done. He called out his troops. Salesmen and mechanics combed the freeways and surface roads of Maverick in their fleet cars and trucks. In more expensive Chevys the rest of us, with the exception of Helen, who stayed at home and manned the phones under armed guard, went to check out John Paul's known haunts and hang-outs. Bob took Suzette and me and a modest shotgun in the Silverado. Kristen had the pleasure of Jerry Mountain's company. Every search vehicle had a mobile. The searchers were told not to approach John Paul under any circumstances if they saw the yellow car but to call Bob and Travis Holbien, though I had my doubts whether Kristen had any intention of doing that.

She and Jerry went to an expensive strip of bars and nightclubs on Ransom Avenue, while we raced over to New Plantation – no sign, dark house – before taking up the solemn task of touring the parking lots of every gentleman's club, as Bob called them, on the west side of town.

Bonaparte's, Sodom'n'Gomorrah's, the Aztec Club, the Weird West, Byron's, Byzantium, President's, Le Stiff – we saw a lot of architecture clumsily reminiscent of ancient civilisations and the Belle Époque, but no little yellow car. The milky evening light dimmed; the ostentatious lights of the titty bar façades came on without any sighting of John Paul.

One of the many calls – the call waiting light was on almost continually – did raise our hopes briefly, it's true. A spray paint specialist called Larry Clemons was in hot pursuit of the Haiku on Highway 79 . . . until he realised he was chasing a particularly ragged taxi on its way to Maverick World Airport.

As the desperate hours went by and the mood inside the Silverado became numb, even Suburban Bob became pessimistic. I began to pay more and more attention to Quiknews, the AM station Bob had put on, low volume, as soon as he'd fired up the Silverado at Logan Hollow. I felt tenser every time the modulating news headlines rolled around. It was increasingly easy to imagine John Paul Mountain as a breaking story.

By ten o'clock we had almost exhausted Bob's oddly abundant knowledge of the topless hotspots of Maverick. 'There's just one more place I can think of he might have gone. Rise and Fall on Dasher Avenue. But this is really our Hail Mary pass.'

I nodded seriously, reasonably sure I knew what he was talking about.

'I've been praying for some time,' Suzette muttered from back of the extended cab.

We headed north on the Beltway, passing the honeycombs of light within the office blocks of the old Consort District, everything swept by the Tower's snow-white beam. Traffic and weather reports on Quiknews swept by every ten minutes. I soon grew to detest the flourish of liquid violins that heralded the traffic status report, read at auctioneer-speed by one Marcie Jungeblut, who made the Roadkill gal sound like a drunk. But as the Silverado curved eastwards in moderate traffic, one item from her chant stood out like a spike:

'I-29 the Splendora freeway outbound at Logan Hollow, hit and run involving a taxi blocking the two left lanes, trapped passenger, Sky Angel on its way.'

The only thing said was a soft 'Oh, Jesus' from Suzette. With all the gravity and urgency of Air Force One turning for home, Bob diverted the Silverado and sped sensibly to the scene of the accident.

The tailback began almost as soon as we got on I-29. A grim-looking Bob took the next exit and we continued up the feeder road, frustrated by other freeway refugees and frequent red lights. Bob made one laconic phone call, to Helen, telling her to expect a bad result, but not to alarm Kristen just yet. He fielded many more calls from his dealership team, starting with Steve Dildine, telling them all to call off the search. 'I believe we've found him,' he said each time.

We saw the attendant lights of the accident as far away as I'd seen the giant dealership flag that first day in Maverick. Orange flashes filled the air. 'How many . . . ambulances?' I asked.

'Those are just the wreckers,' Bob replied quietly.

I counted eight tow-trucks, each with its crown of busy lights, as we edged along the feeder towards the wreck itself. Then the even more intense lights of police cruisers – red, blue, electric white – came into view. Then I did see an ambulance, and caught a glimpse of yellow wreckage.

Bob said, 'We need to park this thing.'

He barnstormed his way across two lanes into the parking lot of a supermarket called Plenty.

Switching off the ignition, Bob turned to both me and Suzette. 'Are you sure you're up for this?'

'He's my brother,' she replied simply.

Suzette and I held hands as we followed close behind Bob. He jogged heavily to the nearest red light on the feeder road – to cross anywhere else would have been suicide. Once on the freeway side we climbed up a grass bank, Bob slipping once and fraying the knee of his trousers. We clambered over the barrier and ran along the shoulder; it was crunchy with orange and red tail-light fragments. As we passed the last of the wreckers, a darkly uniformed cop – how many police forces did they have in this city? – caught sight of us and walked forward to block our path with a no-nonsense look on his face.

'How can I help you, folks?'

'What kind of car is that up there, officer?' Bob demanded.

'It *was* a Haiku.'

Suzette turned away. I couldn't.

'And not a taxi?' Bob asked.

'Wasn't carrying any passengers if he was.'

'That's my son-in-law you're talking about,' Bob replied with bitter dignity.

The cop's attitude changed.

'Sorry to keep you back like this. Thought you were rubberneckers. These days some people even get out of their cars to get a better look. I'll bring you as close as you can go.'

We followed the brisk officer down the remaining slope of the overpass we were on. Past another wrecker and two cruisers we saw the car clearly, what was left of it. I recognised it the way you might still technically recognise a friend beaten to a pulp.

The cop told us what he knew:

According to witnesses, the driver of the Haiku had slammed on his brakes – apparently for no reason – and had been violently rear-ended by a black SUV, which sent him careening into the concrete barrier. The SUV itself fled the scene after a brief stop further along the hard shoulder: the Haiku driver had been the victim (the cop's word) of a hit and run.

I could see a star of cracked windshield where he must have hit his head. Emergency workers were gathered around the driver's side like the service team of a Formula One car. Our cop stopped us, gently, parallel with the redundant ambulance.

'We've got to keep things clear for the Sky Angel,' said another cop, in yet another law enforcement uniform. 'They're about to take him out.'

'How bad is it?' Suzette asked.

Our cop grimaced. 'It's bad, miss. They're having to use the Jaws of Life. But he is alive. Not conscious, but alive.'

By now John Paul's accident – if that's what it was – had shut down both sides of the freeway. I held Suzette and Suzette held me, the drone of a rescue-vehicle generator excusing our silence. The grinding sound made me think of the compressor back in the collision centre; this was one car, surely, that they would write off.

All we could see of John Paul was a still figure tilted back in his seat, looking more like a crash-test dummy than a human being. For some reason the paramedic leaning over him reminded me of a make-up artist preparing a chat-show guest.

Then – softly, softly – they pulled him clear and lowered him onto a waiting stretcher. He was like a man emerging from earthquake rubble.

Seeing John Paul on that stretcher, it was hard to believe he was still alive. Most of his skull was embalmed in a moulded bandage, one that must have been specially designed for serious head wounds. Those parts of him that were not covered looked rubbery – an arm, a cheek, his lips. The entourage of emergency workers spirited him into the fat belly of the Sky Angel. The ambulance crew came back down the ramp immediately, hunched over, as the two on-board medics fluently closed the wide back doors of the helicopter.

Within seconds the craft nudged forward and was airborne at a sharp angle, gaining altitude with abandon. I couldn't help but think of his father's fear of flying.

The helicopter's swooshing roar was soon no more, as the Sky Angel headed in the direction of the Gastec Tower – I discovered that it had, after all, renamed itself in my imagination – the Gastec Tower and its snow-white beam, the craft's own lights pulsing.

The accident was already in the clearing stages.

Part Four

BEYOND MAVERICK

For once the *Sunday Sybarite* wasn't exaggerating: St Attracta's Church, Dublin 4, *was* packed to capacity. The turn-out took me by surprise, but really it shouldn't have. I should have remembered that Dubliners are wonderful about death. The dignity that he had failed to regain in life would now be accorded to him. In death he was a new man.

It was also convenient that the large church was jam-packed. Arriving a little late – I had chauffeured Maurice Swarbrigg from the Law Library and his bulk seemed to weigh down my car – we found it was standing room only. But I was content to lurk at the very back, by the wooden rack of guidance pamphlets.

I was less surprised that he was being buried as a Catholic. Dying intestate – what really was there to leave behind? – he had left no specific instructions about his funeral. That vacuum the Church filled energetically. She is seasoned in the business of dying; the renegade is always a novice.

Jerry's first cousin, Father Dermot Mountain, SJ, conducted the funeral Mass, flanked by two white lines of concelebrants, enough, as my old master whispered to me, 'for a seven-a-side rugby match, with substitutes'.

Suzette, looking darkly regal in her funeral suit, rose to do the Old Testament reading. Before genuflecting she touched the glossy coffin. She read with brittle clarity, as if she were picking her way through the Tridentine Latin she so admired.

It wasn't until the end of Mass proper that her brother got up to speak.

*   *   *

He suffered American injuries: contusions, lacerations, trauma. Three hours they worked on him in the ER, while we encamped in the lobby of South-west Presbyterian. Its swank was such that I had to keep on reminding myself we were in a hospital, not a hotel. The young women behind the marble reception desk wore prim suits. Porters ferried luggage on trolleys with brass racks. The fountain in front of our semicircle of plush sofas featured a spouting bronze dolphin. I would not have been surprised to hear the sounds of a palm court orchestra wafting out of the cafeteria.

Helen had been waiting for us when we arrived; Kristen and Jerry, whom she had tenderly alerted by phone, arrived minutes later. That was a difficult scene, such a tangle of mixed emotions and half-formed questions, cross-pollinations of love and artful concern. At first I was moved by Jerry's moist eyes, a thick stew, it seemed, of remorse, tenderness, and fear, but, without showing it, I eventually grew weary of that confessional face, Jerry's generous pity for his endangered son, the rest of us, and, of course, himself.

What had I ever seen in this man, these people? What had I ever found sexy in their mess? Their family romance led, directly or indirectly, to the twisted metal of a cheap car most suspiciously crashed and the ICU of an opulent foreign hospital.

Kristen's tears I had more time for, but Kristen I could not look at, not squarely in the eye, at least.

From my distant position I couldn't see any damage on John Paul's face.

He hadn't touched the coffin or genuflected, but at the lectern he was more at home than his sister had been. He began by saying, 'We all knew him as Jerry, but today I would like to remember my father,' and, from that moment on, I could sense that he had the congregation in the palm of his hand. Apart from a few jokes at the expense at the now extinct Serious Radicals, John Paul said nothing about his father's public life, nothing about his family's crises, and nothing about his mother. The eulogy was simply about the kind of father Jerry had been when he and Suzette were children – entertaining, exciting, loving. It was all firmly in the past tense.

First the good news, then the bad. Four hours into our vigil, the surgeon who had operated on John Paul emerged. Charles D. Coneway, face and a beard like an elderly Shakespeare. He and Bob shook hands first; they knew each other by reputation, these prominent Maverickians. Before he gave his status report Bob introduced him, and the doctor shook hands with, in turn, the patient's wife, father, sister, mother-in-law, and friend. With my weak title, I felt uncomfortably irrelevant.

We all sat down, even Bob, and listened to what Dr Coneway had to say. He couldn't have made a better start: 'He's going to make it.'

Jerry clasped his hands as if the Lord had deservedly answered his prayers. A tiny smile appeared on Kristen's otherwise hazy face. Dr Coneway then gave us a necessary dose of clichés:

'He's not out of the woods yet, of course. He has a long road ahead of him, and he's going to need all the support he can get.'

'He'll get it, he'll get it,' Jerry intoned. It sounded like a threat. It didn't interrupt the doctor for long:

'That was a very nasty crash. I've seen many others in similar accidents where drivers have not survived. It's too soon to say just what repercussions those head injuries will have.'

'Head injuries?' Kristen asked foggily.

'Yes. He hit the windshield.' I felt Suzette flinch. 'I'm afraid this stands as a sobering example of what happens when you don't have any restraint on.'

'He wasn't wearing his seat belt?' Suzette asked, with a lick of incredulity.

'No,' I replied.

I knew many eyes were watching me as I stared down at the green swirls in the white marble. I didn't look up until I felt them letting my answer go.

Dr Coneway concluded by saying, 'I know that our consultant post-trauma neurologist, Dr Harvey, will be able to tell you a lot more about that.' He stood up. 'Well, I'm sure you need some time to yourselves.'

'When can we see him, Doctor?' Helen asked, speaking for more significant others.

Coneway smiled charitably. 'In a little while. We're still getting him comfortable. But *immediate* immediate family only,' he added archly. 'This is very, very soon.' He ended with a conciliatory 'I'll send somebody down,' and headed back to the wide bank of elevators behind us.

There wasn't much time for even a strained kind of celebration. Our next visitor arrived within minutes – Travis Holbien.

'How's the boy doing?' he asked.

Bob told him what we knew.

'That's great, but he may not be out of the woods yet.'

'So we've been told,' Jerry said with ministerial hauteur.

'I mean legally,' Officer Holbien explained tersely as he fixed Jerry with his halo stare; the minister resigned.

'Legally?' Suzette prompted.

'Yes, ma'am. In relation to his blood-alcohol level. Plus,' – here he hesitated, whether from reticence or for effect I don't know – 'they recovered that weapon that y'all told me about. There may well be charges, I'm afraid.'

'Well, thanks very much for sharing the information,' Jerry said.

Holbien looked at Bob. 'Under the circumstances I should think they won't ask for a search warrant.'

'A search warrant for what?' Suzette demanded.

'His blood,' Kristen answered numbly.

'Jesus,' Jerry muttered. 'What a country.'

'Don't you understand my brother is the *victim* here?' Suzette added.

Officer Holbien answered by looking exclusively at Kristen. 'The weapons violation is the one to worry about. I'd say you'd best consult a lawyer.'

'I'm gonna call Ted Huffmeister and get him down here right now,' Bob announced.

Holbien excused himself with clipped courtesy. He and Bob walked towards the front door. In the foyer Bob shook his hand and clasped his elbow, extracting from him a few moments' more counsel. He then took out his mobile and headed for a quiet niche. Coming back over to the sofas he said, 'Huff's on his way.' He sat down and put a thick arm around Kristen, another round Suzette. 'It'll be taken care of. I promise you. That's one thing you don't have to worry about.'

A young doctor appeared, a Dr Matheny, his face as chiselled as Dr Coneway's was wrinkled. 'He's stable in ICU,' he said with a carefully calibrated smile.

'Has he regained consciousness yet?' Kristen asked.

Dr Matheny tightened his smile further to a guardedly optimistic grimace. 'No, he's . . . comfortable.'

Jerry looked at me. I knew he wanted to ask how his son could be comfortable if he was unconscious. But, for once, Jerry Mountain held his tongue.

'Now,' Dr Matheny continued, 'I believe we have Mr Mountain's wife, father, and sister here.'

As she got to her feet, Suzette pulled me up by the arm. 'This is my fiancé,' she said, 'John Paul's best friend.'

I didn't contradict her. Dr Matheny scrutinised me.

'We'll wait down here,' Helen said, putting her arm around her husband's broad back.

Dr Matheny had finished his deliberation. 'OK,' he said, 'but only briefly. This is still a delicate time.'

So the four of us followed the doctor to the intensive care unit. In the stretcher-wide lift, Kristen and I looked at each other, perhaps the first human look we had given each other since the Hill Country.

I was surprised by how small the room was. Indeed, everything on this fourth floor looked far more modest, more public ward, than the polished lobby downstairs had promised. Inside we did make quite a crowd. I could understand Dr Matheny's concern that we didn't stay too long. He hovered to one side of us. A nurse in light turquoise trousers and tunic was fine-tuning John Paul's tubes, drips, and high-tech guardians. His head, now without that shell they'd put on him at the accident site, looked soft and vulnerable. His face was pale and boyish, brows tracked with stitches, forehead smudged with bruises.

Suzette and I locked tense arms around each other. Kristen walked to the bed and put her hands on the aluminium rail, looking down at her comatose husband as if she were peering into a muddy pool of ornamental fish. Nurse and doctor exchanged a professional glance.

Jerry walked forward a few steps, not going as close to the bed as Kristen, and said quietly, 'I'm sorry, son. I'm sorry. I'm sorry. I'm sorry.' He turned around. That expression I had seen before, on the faces of prominent men who had just been given a fair yet catastrophic sentence, a look you never get to see in the media because by the time they leave court their faces are shielded by newspapers or splayed hands.

Jerry Mountain looked as if he had finally been found guilty.

When the Mass was over, the undertaker's men wheeled the coffin swiftly down the aisle – no pallbearers for Jerry – the tightly packed congregation rising as it passed, shielding me from the chief mourners. When Maurice and I eventually made it through the cram in the porch, numerous small groups of good-humoured mourners were standing around in the cold, overcast early June morning. Amid those knots of influence I spotted two former taoisigh, the current taoiseach's aide-de-camp, a Nobel Laureate, a rock star, a transvestite, several Jesuits, a girl that both John Paul and Jerry were rumoured to have slept with, and a slew of faded television personalities: the walls of Bunny Farrell's bar come to life. But the most significant people I saw were Nessa's parents, John Paul and Suzette's surviving grandparents. Those slim octogenarians were to me the very picture of dignity, though perhaps from another angle all I would have seen was dazed frailty.

I wanted to go over and pay my respects, but something held me back. The same reserve had afflicted me when I heard Jerry was in a private nursing home (that Bermuda account never quite ran dry), dying of the colon cancer he'd seemed to have beaten. I stayed away, but his son – his real son – didn't. John Paul and his supportive wife flew into Dublin days before he died; or, in one version of the story I heard, just hours. Either way, John Paul was at his father's deathbed. Maverick – my Maverick – had done that much.

He slipped by us and left the room. I softly excused myself – as if I were leaving a chapel – and followed him, feeling a form of relief to be away from the sleeping, smashed John Paul. Indeed, part of me still felt I had no right to be there in the first place. Jerry had marched almost all the way back to the elevator bank by the time I caught up with him, arms stiffly by his side, fists clenched, and disappearing into the sleeves of that by now well-wrinkled summer suit.

'Mr Mountain,' I called out formally, perhaps because the sight of him bordered on the pathetic. Besides, hadn't he gone by that name, Jerry, too much of his life? Hadn't he denied himself the dignity of other names – father, friend – too often?

He turned around, puzzled.

I touched the arm of his jacket lightly. 'I just thought I'd come down with you.'

I walked forward and hit the down button. Jerry was nodding seriously to himself. 'Comfortable. Yes, he does look comfortable.'

'As comfortable as he could,' I replied, 'under the circumstances.'

'Yes,' he nodded, 'under the circumstances.'

Mercifully the elevator doors opened, revealing an empty chamber. Inside, I pressed the button marked *One*.

'I think you'll find we're going to the ground floor,' Jerry rumbled.

How to handle this? With as much tact as I could muster. 'Eh, actually Jerry, over here the first floor is the ground floor.'

He breathed in noisily, then raised a pair of mortified eyebrows. 'I see.'

I wished I hadn't corrected him.

In the lobby, Helen was sitting forward on one of the couches, hands and knees clustered together. Bob, standing, was talking to a shorter man. They turned around when they heard Jerry approach over the marble. I heard Bob's companion being introduced as Ted Huffmeister. He was a compact man with a Germanic face and steel-grey hair and moustache. Jerry shook his hand for a long time, muttering about privilege. Then I was introduced, Bob telling the lawyer I was his 'Irish counterpart', and, with a wink to me, as 'our QB'. I smiled ignorantly back.

But I did know one thing for certain. Everything would be taken care of, everything was under control, legally at least.

And indeed, months later, I heard that John Paul got off lightly, got deferred adjudication. Deferred adjudication is not exactly guilt, but neither is it innocence. It's just something they have in America.

Maurice Swarbrigg, who had been paying his respects to a disgraced judge, now paraded back to where I was standing.

'Quite a turn-out,' he said.

'Yes indeed.'

'If he'd had this number of first-preference votes last time he ran for the Dáil he would have been re-elected.'

I was not in the mood to hear this. For once I didn't want to hear jokes told at Jerry's expense. The Mountains were no laughing matter any more.

'Maurice,' I said, 'do you think you could get a lift back into town with Justin Boru?'

'What's wrong with your car?'

'Nothing. It's just that – it's just that I think I'll follow the cortège out to the cemetery.'

Mirth invaded Maurice's wide, pock-marked face. 'You want to see him go under! Well really, Dagg, I knew you had it in for these Mountains, but this is going far beyond the call of duty. And you know, I don't believe I can think of anything better to do with the rest of the morning than do the same. Then we could go down to the Lighthouse for some prawns and still make it back—'

For the first time in my legal life I interrupted a Senior Counsel.

'No, Maurice. I'm sorry, but this is something I'd like to do on my own. It has nothing to do with pleasure.'

Maurice Swarbrigg looked genuinely puzzled. He put his swollen face closer to mine. 'Then what has it to do with? You're not sorry he's dead, surely to goodness?'

I sighed for patience. 'I just have to see this thing through to the end, that's all.'

With a contemptuous smile, Maurice shook his head and, without saying another word, turned around and sauntered over to a gaggle of barristers which included Justin Boru, another of his old devils. Justin Boru would oblige. And Peter Dagg would be doing fewer leaves-for-appeal for a while.

John Paul regained consciousness early the next morning. Kristen,

Suzette and Bob were at the hospital when the news came through, Helen having driven Jerry and me back to Logan Hollow sometime after midnight. We left again with no thought of breakfast. In the pre-rush hour traffic it took us less than fifteen minutes to make it back to the Medical District.

Jerry, in particular, was full of anxious anticipation. Several times he said, 'He'll see things clearly now, he'll see them clearly.'

But this was no great awakening. John Paul was like a man solemnly submerged in a bath. Twice he opened his eyes and gasped, hey. But he didn't seem to hear anything we said. Kristen, who never took her own hand off his unbandaged one, said that he had been about the same since first opening his eyes at five-thirty.

A nurse came in and politely advised us that we couldn't have this many people in the room. Suzette and I volunteered to go on a coffee run to the cafeteria. As we were leaving John Paul suddenly spoke:

'Peter,' he croaked.

I turned around. His eyes were wide open, his flaky lips forming a smile.

'Yes, John Paul?' I said solicitously.

He slid his hand out from underneath his wife's, and pointed an unsteady finger at me.

'Bang, bang.'

His eyelids drooped down again, but the smile remained for a few seconds longer. I was the new centre of attention in that little room.

Grunting a laugh, I turned around again and walked out.

Going down in the lift, Suzette asked:

'What was the bang, bang business about, then?'

I sighed. 'I have no idea.'

Suzette frowned at the changing floor numbers.

'Peter, how did you know he had a gun in the first place?'

I raised my eyebrows until I had an answer in place.

'I work with criminals, dear. I know these things.'

The air in the elevator chilled.

'My brother is no criminal.'

'Sorry. Didn't mean to imply that.'

I wasn't sure whether I was lying or not.

A dull bell sounded and the door opened on the first floor.

'Funny it was you, of all people, he talked to first,' Suzette said, walking out.

'Yes, funny,' I replied, following her.

I was the last car in the cortège, which was much shorter than the size of the congregation had led me to expect. Official Dublin, Celebrity Dublin, had done its bit: the public man had been rehabilitated; his burial was a private matter: it was family business. Since I was less than ten cars behind the hearse, I stayed as far back as the ordinary traffic would allow, wondering if I shouldn't do the sensible thing – a U-turn. But I kept on following the Mountains.

I felt more comfortable when we got onto a stretch of motorway – no longer a novelty in Ireland – that ran towards the dark purple pyramid of the Sugar Loaf; the hearse driver picked up the pace, exceeding the speed limit at one point. I had not been this far south in County Dublin for several years, and so I was surprised by the intensity of development going on; the city was pinning itself up against its hills.

But the type of development – *that* I recognised, that I had seen before. Behind fresh granite walls, billboards presented visions of the communities that would soon flourish on mucky construction sites: Tara Court, Chieftain's Wood, Deirdre's Lake, the Glen of the Monks, the Old Demesne.

No, I was not tempted to buy property in any of those unreal Irelands. After Maverick, I had done a token amount of work on the hovel that was to have been our nuptial nest, and sold it for a shameful profit. I actually phoned Suzette – the first, tentative words we had exchanged since Texas – and offered her half the equity. She killed the call.

Since then the money had been in the bank, while I half-heartedly looked around for a place to buy, a place for myself alone. At times I felt as if I had financial constipation, but still I couldn't opt for the quick catharsis of a place in the outer suburbs. A year has passed since my Maverick misadventures, and I am still in my cosy Ballsbridge cell. Perhaps I will just blow the entire fifty grand on a brand-new BMW.

When the motorway ended the cortège slowed to a more funereal pace. It passed a stonemason's yard – the dense display of headstones making me think of Nessa, buried in her Père Lachaise compartment – and turned left into Rathdown Cemetery. On top of the walls ran the layer of black spikes I had read about in the *Sunday Sybarite* some weeks ago: a response by the local council to the persistent theft of flowers and vases. The *Syb* blamed local heroin addicts.

I suspected that until his downfall Jerry had notions that he would one day be buried alongside Ireland's other great liberators in the maturity of Glasnevin. As it was, he would lie beside obscure suburbanites in a cemetery so new that one half of it, to the left of the treeless avenue, was as yet entirely undug. And I could see, as I parked my car at the far end of the lot, that there was plenty of room for development on the right too.

I waited until all the other mourners had got out of their cars and followed the coffin into the graveyard proper. I was tempted to put the key back in the ignition – surely I'd done enough and seen enough – to drive away undetected. But the words I'd spoken to Maurice Swarbrigg came back to me, and I knew that I did have to see this thing through to the end, whatever the consequences.

I got out of the car and walked as far as the cinder-block structure that housed the cemetery office and the toilets. I stood near an old woman filling a watering can from an outside tap and scanned the young cemetery. There was no other burial in progress, no other group of mourners I could pretend to be a part of. The Mountain funeral was my funeral.

And so, hands deep in the black greatcoat I was glad I had worn, more for the illusion of camouflage it gave me than the cold, I started to walk through the graveyard. Though I paused every so often to look at the headstone of one of the recent dead, as if I might have been looking for a friend, I was sidling ever closer to the ring of no more than two dozen people that had formed at the end of an incomplete row.

Now that John Paul was out of danger, the time had come to take care of some business that had nothing to do with him, and everything.

On the third evening after the accident, I suggested to my fiancée that we take a quiet walk around Logan Hollow. She said she would like that. You see, I'd learned how to do this from all the girls who'd broken up with me over the years, usually after a week or so. Giving her the bullet – that had been the Berchmans slang for this act. To give her the bullet, you picked a quiet spot, a quiet moment.

After a few blocks of small talk, I slowed us to a halt in front of a generic red-brick mansion, the grass blades of its infallible lawn standing to regimental attention.

I said it quickly, in words that I chose not to record, not because they were cruel – pointedly they were not – but because of the cruelty they implied. Here I chose to let my memory, my faithful internal stenographer, fail me.

But I cannot forget Suzette's mortally wounded stare, the accusing chorus of rhythmic insects in the background, or her eventual reply:

'You couldn't wait till we got back to Dublin to tell me this?'

'No, no I couldn't – that's the point. Back in Dublin we'll get back into the old ways, the old positions – no matter what restaurant by Daire ffrench-Brady we're sitting in. I don't trust myself in Dublin.'

Suzette glared at me.

'I trusted you in Dublin, Peter.'

I couldn't look at her any more. At last I felt ashamed – clear, pure shame. What was I doing to her? The last thing she needed was somebody letting her down, abandoning her – first her mother, then her brother, now me. Losing people – that was the Mountain disease.

So I felt shame, but not enough guilt to break my resolve. Something ruthless in me had emerged, some fight-or-flight mechanism. Or perhaps, in my case, a fight-and-flight mechanism. I always had it in me, I suspect, but had only discovered it in the hard light of Maverick.

'I'm sorry, I'm sorry, I'm sorry,' I said, shaking my head, looking down at the fibrous Maverick grass, so different to our own sweet and docile blades back home, the old sod indeed.

But my worst line was still in store: 'Why don't you keep the ring?'

It came off her finger with surprising ease. And her aim was surprisingly accurate – she hit me in the temple.

So who had given who the bullet?

In the end, I got close enough to recognise Tom Iremonger, and to see him putting a strong arm around his fiancée, Suzette Mountain; and to hear Father Mountain's insistent, nasal prayers; and to see the brassy edge of Jerry Mountain's coffin as it was lowered into the black ground.

I had expected that I would turn around and start walking back to my car before the graveside mourners started to peel away. But I didn't move: I froze between two strangers' headstones.

When Suzette saw me, she stared for a moment, more in astonishment than contempt, I think, then made some rapid comment to her fresh fiancé. He looked over and gave me an oily smile. Suzette was marrying a man who had put his wild past behind him, abruptly. Iremonger was now one of the new mobile moguls. His company, Ire-Com, had just won, and not without controversy, one of the latest service provider licences. So now both Mountain children had found their way back to money. (Too late for Jerry, alas.) Tom Iremonger was worth fifteen million, on paper at least. I nodded back, hoping that I would one day have the pleasure of prosecuting him or, even better, defending him.

The last days of Maverick were a polite hell.

An hour after I had ended the future with Suzette, Kristen tiptoed up to me in the pool room – I was busy losing to myself – and asked, so very reasonably, if I would mind terribly if she brought over the rest of my belongings from the guest bedroom at New Plantation, as my ex-fiancée would now be staying with her until John Paul came home.

I did mind terribly.

I said, 'That would be no problem.'

Suzette was not the only person pleased with the new sleeping arrangements: her father, who neither asked nor was told about our estrangement, immediately saw me as a partner-in-crime. The first night he woke me up at 2 a.m. to tell me that he'd dialled up a pay-per-view porn movie on the giant TV in the Pentagon. (I wouldn't have minded a look, but not with Jerry there.) After Bob and Helen – pre-dawn risers – had retreated to their house-within-a-house master bedroom, Jerry would break open bottles of Veuve Clicquot and Jack Daniels, lifted from their abundant bar. Another night he took a Venetian glass ashtray that caught his eye; Jerry didn't smoke. And I swear the aftershave he wore one morning was the same as Bob's.

In Dublin he had never been such a petty thief.

I saw John Paul twice more in hospital after breaking up with Suzette. Both times he was awake, and both times he barely acknowledged any Dubliner's presence. Add to that my awkwardness with his sister and his wife and you had a festival of resentment.

Clearly I had overstayed my welcome in Maverick. Not that Bob and Helen said anything. They remained the ideal hosts, despite the strain of coping with broken John Paul and his broken entourage. But that very perfection was my cue that it was high time I went home, or to the changed home I had created while I was away.

So, five days after the accident, with my former brother-in-law-to-be out of the ICU, I cancelled my original return date and booked a seat on a flight leaving for Dublin, via Newark, at seven the following morning.

Bob insisted on driving me to Maverick World Airport. He pulled up suavely at the set-down area, then looked across at me with a fond grimace.

'Well, Coach, looks like you're a free agent.'

He held out a sure hand; I shook it.

'That I am, Bob. That I am.'

'But come back and see us any time you want. Any time you're passing through Maverick.'

'I will.' But I knew that I would never return, and regretted it. 'Thank Helen for me again. You two have been most kind – to all of us. Thanks for everything.'

'Any time, Coach. Any time.'

Behind his smile I thought I detected a little impatience. This was after all the hour he usually got to the dealership. So I shook his hand once again, jumped down from the Silverado, and retrieved my larger bag from the bed of the truck. Bob waved casually as he drove off. A hot wind was blowing in the grey light. I marched towards the terminal's mild climate.

Here came the Wingate-Mountains – in grief, in Dublin, looking more like a couple than they ever had in Maverick. And Kristen, I had to admit, was looking magnificent. In her tight black suit and dark glasses she was worthy of a Kennedy funeral; I hoped that wherever Jerry was, if he was anywhere at all, he could at least see her, his hard-won daughter-in-law.

I cannot say that Kristen ignored me or simply failed to notice me. Kristen was incapable of noticing me because I was not in the same biosphere as her; just one anti-glance from those dark glasses told me that.

But John Paul saw me. John Paul saw me and started striding my way.

Jolted, I couldn't help but think of the ice cream van lot, that other graveyard, and for a moment I wondered if I should take cover behind one of the headstones, just in case.

But his purpose this time wasn't as straightforward as murder. Disturbingly, he came in peace. With a mild smile, he held out his hand. After a hesitation, I shook it, formally.

'Thank you for coming, Peter. It was good of you.'

I did not want to affirm that, in relation to his family, anything was good of me. So I said what my parents always said at funerals, 'I'm sorry for your trouble,' and wished I hadn't when I saw his eyebrows rise in detached delight, and remembered just how much trouble I had to be sorry for.

So I added, 'You're looking well, John Paul, under the circumstances.'

He smiled at the half-lie, revealing teeth as flawless as a baby set; only American dentistry could have worked that miracle. But now I could see that his face was not so perfect. You could make out the faultlines of the reconstructive surgery above his brow and around his nose and ears. The skin had been pulled tight across his cheeks and jowls, giving him back, in an exaggerated way, the jawline he used to have in his dissolute Dublin days.

'But, Peter, do you know exactly what the circumstances are?'

I shook my head. 'No, John Paul. I can't say I know as much about your family as you do.'

'Well, that's a change. But anyway, I thought you'd be interested to hear that I'm out of the car business.'

'Really. Did someone make you an offer you couldn't refuse?'

'Truck Nation made my father-in-law an offer he couldn't refuse. Bob's staying on for another three years was the dealmaker, but between you and me he spends half his day in the shop now.'

I nodded. 'It's nice to have work one loves. But what about you, John Paul? You weren't tempted to stay on the bridge?'

'Oh, let's just say I have other interests now.'

'You're not working on a memoir, are you?'

'Don't be ridiculous, Peter. No, looks like I'll be going into business with my brother-in-law. Tom Iremonger, I mean.'

'I know who you mean. Does this mean we'll be seeing more of you in Dublin?'

'Perhaps. I'm more a silent partner. We'll be dividing our time between here and there. A lot of it depends on Kristen's work. She's almost got her doctorate, you know.'

'Glad to hear it. And glad to see you're not so allergic to Dublin any more.'

I thought he would react to that jab, but instead he looked delighted. He said, 'You know, Peter, that's the real reason I came over to talk to you – to thank you.'

I did not like that serene tone of voice.

'You don't have to thank me, John Paul.'

'Oh but I do. We all do.'

'We?'

'Yes. Myself, my sister, my wife. Even my poor father.'

Behind him workers were putting a rough canopy over the grave. But for that, I would have smiled.

I said, 'You mean I did your dirty work.'

His scarred brow wrinkled. 'Well, I think you did your own dirty work too, my friend. But we won't dwell on that. No, what I mean is that without you I might still be in Maverick. I might still be stuck in that . . . phase.'

A phase – that's all it was? A phase? Well, of course it was.

I sighed. 'Someone had to bring you to your senses, John Paul.'

This didn't bother him either. 'And my sister picked the right man for the job. The softly-softly man.'

'Please don't mention it.'

'Perhaps you should do that kind of thing more often, Peter. Could be your true vocation.'

I shook my head. 'I'm done with devilling.'

His reorganised face looked briefly puzzled. Then he slapped me on the shoulder – a Maverick slap – and said, 'I'd better catch up with my family. I'd ask you to lunch in the Lighthouse if I thought there was any chance of you accepting.'

Was there any chance of me accepting? No. But did I wish he had used that kind of excuse the day I had hovered outside the Cloud House? No again. My dance around the Mountains might have been foolish, but it had made me what I was.

John Paul turned and walked briskly to catch up with the retreating mourners. I walked slowly over to his father's grave. As I looked at the displaced mat of turf and the ready mound of earth, I wondered how soon the gravediggers would complete their job. They were nowhere to be seen now. Had they gone off to have their lunch, just like the funeral party? Daydreaming, I imagined the Mexican labourers of Logan Hollow doing the job for them. Looking up, I saw the black Mercedes containing my quartet of ex-friends rolling out of the cemetery. My eye fell again on the crude canopy of planks covering the mouth of the grave. I remembered his handshake, that ancient day – remembered feeling, for as long as it lasted, like someone of consequence.

Well, now I was someone.

I turned away, leaving the Mountains to rest in whatever peace they could find.